Bedtime Stories For Kids

A Collection of Short, Funny,

Fantasy Stories to Help

Children & Toddlers Fall Asleep

Fast, and Have a Relaxing Night's Sleep

By
Amelia Roberts

TABLE OF CONTENTS

Introduction:
Fantastic Bedtime Stories For Amazing Dreams

For parents...

There is nothing more soothing than to tell your child a bedtime story before sending them off to sleep. Stories for children are a special way for you to teach wonderful lessons while opening your child's imagination to the endless possibilities of the world.

To make sure that your child sleeps well at night, you should help them create a bedtime routine. This bedtime routine should include relaxing activities like meditation or deep breathing exercises, a relaxing environment (their bedroom), and, of course, a bedtime story. While you prepare the other parts of your child's bedtime routine, this book will cover storytime. Here, you have a collection of bedtime stories about different fantasy creatures. From mermaids, fairies, dragons, and more, your child will feel amazed at all the tales in this book.

The best part is that all of these stories have important moral values for your child to learn. You can either choose a story to enchant your child each night or you can ask your child to choose. Either way, your child will be introduced to a magical world of imaginative events, memorable characters, and heartwarming lessons. Each time you tell a story to your child, take your time. Storytime is a wonderful activity that will strengthen your bond with your child and bring you closer to each other... and this is the perfect book for this purpose.

-

The Importance Of Family

Chapter 1:
The Importance Of Family

Our family is one of the most important treasures we have in the world. But sometimes, children forget the value of family, especially when they feel sad or angry. These stories are all about the unconditional love of family and how children can depend on their families to overcome any challenge in life.

A New Baby on the Way

Venus is a young fairy who lives in a house with her Mom and Dad. Unlike her other fairy friends, she was an only child and she was used to getting everything she wanted from her parents. She loved her parents very much and she listened to them all the time to make them happy. She helped out with chores at home and she did very well in fairy school.

One day, Venus woke up with a smile on her face. Venus jumped out of bed, folded her blanket, and fluttered down to the dining room to have breakfast. But when she got to the dining room, her parents weren't there! All she saw was a plate of fruit and a glass of sparkling water.

"Mom?" Venus called out, "Dad?"

But nobody answered. She fluttered to her parents' room but they weren't there either. So Venus went back to the dining room, sat down, and started eating her breakfast by herself. When she was almost done, her parents came home and both of them had huge smiles on their faces.

"Good morning, Venus!" her Mom said.

"Good morning," said her Dad as he kissed her on the forehead.

"Good morning, Mom and Dad," Venus replied. "Where did you come from?"

"Well," Venus' Dad said as they both sat down next to her, "we just came from the fairy doctor."

"Why?" Venus asked. She felt worried. "Are you sick?"

"Oh, no, dear!" her Mom exclaimed. "In fact, we have wonderful news for you."

"Really?" Venus said. "What is it?"

Her parents looked at each other and exchanged a warm, loving smile. Then they both looked at Venus and her Dad said, "You're going to be a big sister!"

At first, Venus didn't understand what her Dad said. Then she realized that her Mom was going to have another baby!

"Isn't it exciting?" Venus' Mom asked.

The young fairy looked at her parents. They were both smiling with excitement so she said, "Y-yes, that's great news." Venus' parents stood up, gave her a tight hug, then her Dad said, "We'll be in our room if you need us. Mom has to rest."

"Okay," Venus said, "I will go out after breakfast. I'm going to the park."

"Alright," her Mom said, "just be careful. See you later, Venus."

When her parents left, Venus looked at her breakfast. She suddenly lost her appetite. A new baby? She worried about sharing her parents with a baby brother or sister. The more Venus thought about it, the sadder she felt. She was almost about to cry when her Mom fluttered back into the dining room.

"Oh," said her mom, "you're still here, Venus?"

Venus looked up at her Mom and said, "Oh, yes, mom. I was just about to leave."

"Now?" her Mom asked. "But it's almost time for lunch. Your Dad and I thought that you had already left a few hours ago!"

"What?" Venus said as she looked at the clock. Her Mom was right! It was almost lunchtime.

"Are you okay, Venus?" her Mom asked. She sat down next to the young fairy.

"Well," Venus said, "I'm... worried."

"Why?" her Mom asked.

"I'm worried about having a baby brother or sister. I'm scared that you won't love me anymore," Venus said sadly.

"Oh, Venus," said her mom. She gave Venus a tight hug and reassured her, "That will never happen. Your Dad and I love you very much and we have more than enough love to give the little baby too."

"Really?" Venus asked.

"Yes," her Mom replied, "in fact, it will be wonderful! You will have someone to love and take care of. Someone who will look up to you and see you as the best big sister in the world."

Venus smiled. Now, she knew that having a new baby wasn't a bad thing. Because of her mom's explanation, Venus felt excited about having a new baby brother or sister!

Sibling Fights

Nathan and Troy are two young dragon brothers who enjoyed playing together every day. Nathan is the older brother and Troy is two years younger than him. One day, the dragon brothers went out to play.

"Where are we going, Nathan?" Troy asked.

"Let's go up to the hill. We can have a fire breathing competition there," answered Nathan.

"Again?" Troy asked. "I thought maybe we can go to the forest today. Let's go explore the parts of the forest that we haven't explored yet."

"No, Troy," argued Nathan, "I want to go to the top of the hill. Since I'm the older one, you have to listen to me. Now, wait here while I tell Mom and Dad where we're going."

As Nathan left Troy out in the garden, the young dragon was feeling angry. His brother never listened to him! Troy was so upset that he decided to fly into the forest by himself.

"I'm tired of following Nathan all the time," Troy said to himself. Sometimes, he and Nathan would explore the different parts of the forest together. He knew some parts of the forest but today, he wanted to explore the parts that they haven't been to yet. As Troy explored, he heard a small voice coming from one of the trees. It said, "Hey, dragon! Do you want to see something amazing?"

Troy looked up at the tree and saw a small goblin standing in one of the branches. Troy knew that goblins loved to trick other creatures so he said, "No, thank you. I can explore by myself."

"Oh, come on!" said the goblin who hopped from one branch to another as he followed Troy. "You look like a dragon who is worthy."

Troy looked up at the goblin again and said, "Why should I listen to you? Goblins always trick other creatures."

The goblin's eyes widened and he said, "Do you think I would trick a fearsome dragon? Sure, goblins are tricksters, but we only trick small creatures like fairies and dwarves. Never dragons!"

"Okay," Troy said, "what did you want to show me?"

"Follow me!" said the goblin as he started running towards the forest.

"Hey, wait!" Troy said. He ran after the goblin. He kept running and calling out to the goblin who was very fast. Troy was too focused on the goblin to see the part of the forest where thick vines were hanging from the trees. Troy ran right into the vines and got trapped!

"Hey!" Troy said, "I'm trapped!"

Troy tried to wiggle free but he couldn't move. Then he heard the goblin laughing, "You know what," said the goblin, "you were right! We goblins love to trick other creatures! I am leaving now, good luck!" Then the goblin hopped away while laughing.

Troy tried to wiggle out of the vines again but he couldn't get out. He felt scared. It was already getting dark. Just then, he heard Nathan's voice, "Troy! Where are you?"

"Nathan!" Troy called out. "I'm over here! But be careful, I got trapped in thick vines. Please help me!"

Soon, Troy felt Nathan pulling him free. Being a bigger dragon, Nathan was strong enough to pull his younger brother out of the vines.

"Thank you!" Troy said.

"You're welcome," Nathan answered. "But why would you go into the forest by yourself? You know how dangerous it is!"

"I'm sorry," Troy said, "I really wanted to explore the forest but you don't listen to me."

Nathan looked at his younger brother. He felt bad. If he had only listened to Troy, his younger brother wouldn't have gone into the forest alone. Nathan said, "I'm sorry too. Next time, I will listen to you. We can take turns choosing our activities, okay?"

Troy smiled at his big brother and said, "It's a deal!"

Mom and Dad Save the Day

Ava is a small, pink, and fluffy monster who is very adventurous. Sometimes, her parents tell her that she's too adventurous for her own good! Every morning, after she eats breakfast, she would run out of the house to explore. She explores the forest, the meadows, the caves, and even the mountains.

But even if Ava is very brave, her parents warned her never to go into the bog.

Aside from being very slippery, the bog is a dangerous place for fluffy monsters. There is too much moss in the bog and when the moss gets on the fur of fluffy monsters, it will spread all over their body! This is why Ava's parents always remind her never to go to the bog whenever she would go out to explore.

One day, Ava finished her breakfast and called out to her mom, "I'm going out, mom!"

Ava's Mom peeped out of the kitchen and smiled at her fluffy pink daughter. She said, "Alright, take care and come home before lunch."

"Okay, mom," Ava promised. Then she stepped out into the sunshine and smiled. Ava thought about where she would explore today. She couldn't decide whether she would go into the caves or climb up the mountains. After some thought, Ava decided to go into the caves. She might find something new today.

On her way to the caves. Ava passed by the bog. She stopped for a while and looked at it. Even though her parents warned her of the bog, she didn't understand why she couldn't just explore the area around it. "I won't go into the bog. I will just walk around it then I will go to the caves," Ava whispered to herself. She looked around to see if anyone was watching her.

When Ava saw that nobody was around, she smiled. The adventurous little monster carefully walked into the bog and looked around. There were dead trees all around the bog so it was a bit dark. Ava walked around carefully and looked into the bog itself. She couldn't see much, just dark water. While walking carefully, Ava got lost in her own thoughts. Ava thought she was walking carefully but she didn't see the big rock in front of her. So she tripped over the rock and slipped!

"Ouch!" Ava cried out as she fell into a small puddle.

Ava tried to stand up but her foot was too painful. She tried to crawl out of the puddle but it was too slippery. When Ava looked at her hands, she saw that they were covered in moss and when she looked closely, she saw that the moss was spreading.

"Oh, no," Ava said worriedly. No wonder her parents warned her about the bog. If only she listened to them! Ava looked around but there was nobody there to help her. She felt so helpless that she started to cry. Just then, she heard footsteps coming from far away. Ava sat up straight, took a deep breath, and called out again, "Please! Help me!"

Finally, she heard the footsteps running towards her. Then she saw her parents bursting into the darkness, "Ava!" called out her mom. "Is that you?" her Dad cried out.

"Mom! Dad! Yes, it's me! Please help me!" Ava called out.

Ava's parents carefully walked towards Ava and pulled her out of the puddle. They wrapped her in a blanket and took her home. When they got home, they immediately gave her a bath with hot water to wash the moss off.

"I'm sorry I went to the bog," Ava said shyly.

Her parents looked at her and her dad said, "We told you how dangerous it was. It's a good thing we found you in time."

"Yes," Ava said, "you saved me! And I promise never to go into the bog again."

United We Stand

Whenever giants are around, other creatures shiver in fear. But even if giants seem scary and mean, they are actually shy and gentle. Giants are very loyal and they love their families very much. Josh is one of the youngest giants in Giant Village. Just like other young giants, Josh is sometimes friendly with other creatures. One day, Josh was walking to the marketplace to buy fruits for his family. On his way, he met a group of young centaurs who were sitting around and sharing stories.

Josh walked towards them and said, "Hi! My name is Josh. It's time to meet you all."

The centaurs looked at Josh as a group. Only two of the centaurs smiled at him while the others just stared at Josh without saying anything.

"Do you need something?" asked one of the centaurs.

"Not really," Josh replied. "I am on my way to the marketplace and I just wanted to say hi."

"Okay," said the centaur, "you have said hi to us and now you can go."

"Oh," Josh said while feeling embarrassed. Then he gave them one last smile and continued walking. As he was walking, he heard footsteps catching up to him. When Josh turned around, he saw the centaur who smiled at him. "Hi!" she said.

"Hello," Josh said shyly.

"I'm sorry about my friends," the centaur said as she started walking beside Josh. "By the way, my name is Celine. It's nice to meet you, Josh."

Josh smiled at the friendly centaur. Then he asked, "Why were the other centaurs so mean to me?"

"Oh," Celine said, "it's because of Tantor the Terrible."

"Who?" Josh asked.

"Tantor the Terrible," Celine repeated. "He was a big, mean, and scary giant who destroyed our village. We were still very small when it happened but we remember how scary it was to hear that giant stomping around outside our homes."

"I have never heard that name before," Josh said.

"It's because Tantor the Terrible wasn't from Giant Village," Celine said. "He came from across the sea and he said he was looking for something. He destroyed many villages here. But when he went to Giant Village, he was never heard of again."

"Really?" Josh asked.

"Yes. That is why many creatures here don't treat giants well no matter how young they are," Celine said sadly.

Josh thought about what Celine the centaur told him until he went back home. He went into his house and saw his mom. Then he said, "Mom, have you heard of Tantor the Terrible?"

Josh's Mom looked at him with surprise, "Where did you hear that name, Josh?"

"A met a group of centaurs on my way to the marketplace and one of them told me a story about a giant named Tantor the Terrible who destroyed the different villages here," Josh explained.

His Mom sighed. Then she sat down and said, "Tantor is a giant just like us. But he is from a different village. While the other creatures call him Tantor the Terrible, to us, he is just Tantor."

"Why would he destroy the villages, mom?" Josh asked.

"He didn't mean to, Josh. Tantor was under a magic spell. An evil witch got mad at the king of the giants from Tantor's village. So she cast a spell on him to give giants a bad name," his Mom said sadly.

"Celine told me that when Tantor came here to Giant Village, they never saw him again," Josh said.

"That's true," Josh's Mom replied, "we brought him to a powerful wizard to remove the spell then we sent him home. Poor Tantor, he was so ashamed of what he did!"

"You helped Tantor and protected him?" Josh asked.

"Yes," Josh's mom said, "because that is what families do. Even if your family members make mistakes, you forgive them, especially when they didn't mean what they did. We always have to be united because family is the most important thing in the world."

My Friends
And I

Chapter 2:
My Friends And I

As children grow up, they should get the chance to interact, have fun, and play with their friends. After all, these activities are essential for their growth and development. Whether your child has a lot of friends or they are shy and they seldom talk to others, these stories will help them see the value of friendship.

Meeting New Friends

Rose and her family just moved from a different cove. Before they moved, she didn't have a lot of friends at school. Rose was a very shy mermaid and she often felt jealous whenever she would see other young mermaids playing together. Now that they moved to a new cove, Rose thought that this would be the perfect time to start a new life. She promised herself that she would make new friends on her first day of school.

"Good morning, Rose," her Mom said when she entered the dining room.

"Hello, mom. Hello, Dad," Rose answered.

"Are you ready for your first day at school?" her Dad asked.

"Yes," Rose said excitedly, "I want to make a lot of friends today."

"That sounds great!" exclaimed her Mom.

"Good luck, Rose," her Dad said, "I know you will make a lot of friends because you're so kind and sweet."

Rose smiled at her parents and said, "Thanks, guys."

On the way to school, Rose different kinds of mermaids. There were mermaids of every color swimming in this cove. They had different colored tails, different colored hair, and even different colored skin. In her previous cove, Rose always felt like she stood out because she had wild yellow hair as bright as the sun while all the other young mermaids had pale-colored hair.

As she swam to school, she felt more comfortable. Seeing all the different mermaids gave her confidence. But as soon as she reached the school, she felt shy again. Rose kept trying to greet other mermaids but she couldn't find her voice. Just like in her previous school, she sat down at the very back of the classroom and watched everyone else have fun together.

Just then, a mermaid with silver-colored hair sat next to Rose and said, "Hello! My name is Coral. You're new here, aren't you?"

Rose was surprised. She looked at the young mermaid and saw that she had a big smile on her face. Rose said, "H-hello, Coral. My name is Rose."

"Oh," said Coral, "that's such a pretty name! Isn't a rose a kind of flower on the land?"

"Yes," Rose said as she smiled at Coral. "When my Mom was young, she swam to the surface and made friends with a young human child. Then the human child gave her a rose before she moved to a different village. My Mom kept the rose in a bubble and it's on display in our house."

"Wow," Coral said, "that's such a lovely story!"

Rose smiled at Coral, "Thank you," she said.

Then Coral said, "Wait here, Rose."

She swam towards a group of mermaids and started talking to them. After a while, the group of mermaids looked at Rose. Right away, Rose felt shy again. Talking to Coral was great but she couldn't talk to a whole group of mermaids!

It looked like she didn't have a choice though because the group of mermaids swam towards her. Coral was in front of them and she said, "Guys, this is Rose."

Rose smiled at them shyly and said, "Hi."

Coral pointed to the young mermaids one by one as she said their names, "This is Jane, Tabitha, Mark, Greg, Mindy, and Joan." After Coral introduced them, they all waved at Rose. But before they could talk to each other, the bell rang and their teacher came in.

"Let's talk later, Rose," Coral said as she and the other young mermaids swam to their seats. As Rose watched the other mermaids swim to their seats, she couldn't stop smiling. It was wonderful meeting new friends and she couldn't wait until they could play together and share stories with each other.

Say No To Bullying

The fairies of the forest all lived in peace and harmony. The grown-up fairies worked together to make the Fairy Forest a happy and beautiful place. But the young fairies who were still learning how to be good weren't as peaceful as their parents. While in school, a lot of them would be mean to other fairies, especially the ones who were different.

Vincent was one of those young fairies who looked different from the others. While most of the other fairies had green or brown hair, Vincent had bright red hair. The fairies of the forest all looked the same but once in a while, they welcomed fairies from different lands to live in the forest with them. Vincent and his family were fire fairies which is why they had red hair, silver wings, and gray eyes. Whenever they flew around the forest, they stood out because of their colors.

On his first day of school, Vincent felt scared. He said, "Mom, Dad, do I really have to go to school today?"

"Of course, Vincent," said his Mom with a smile. She knew that Vincent was worried about being teased but she also knew that Vincent was a strong, confident fairy who could stand up for himself.

"Why, Vincent," asked his dad, "are you feeling worried?"

"Yes," Vincent said, "I heard that the young fairies of the forest can be very mean, especially to fairies who don't look like them."

"Well," Vincent's Mom said, "maybe you can change that."

"Your Mom is right," Vincent's Dad agreed, "you are one of the bravest young fairies I know. If anyone can change the minds of the other young fairies, I believe you can."

Vincent smiled at his parents. He knew that they didn't want to leave the fire pit where they came from but unlike other types of fairies, fire fairies had to move from one place to another all their lives. So Vincent put on a brave face, kissed his parents goodbye, and flew to school.

When he reached the fairy school, Vincent saw that most of the young fairies all had brown or green hair and golden wings. Most of them were forest fairies. But he did see some fire, water, and wind fairies here and there. This made Vincent feel more confident. He flew all the way to his classroom and when he went inside, he saw a group of fairies gathered in the corner of the room. Then Vincent realized that they were all surrounding a young fairy. They were laughing at the small fairy saying mean things to her.

Right away, Vincent stood up and walked over to the group of forest fairies. Then he said, "Hey, what's going on here?"

One of the fairies looked at Vincent and said, "Go away fire fairy."

Vincent looked at the blue fairy who sat in the corner. She was hugging her knees and her head was bowed down. He could see that she was a water fairy. Vincent looked at the other fairies and said, "Why are you bullying her? Did she do something wrong to you?"

The other forest fairies looked embarrassed except for the one who looked like the leader of the group. He said, "Why do you care?"

"I'm different, just like her. If you want to bully someone, you can bully me," Vincent said bravely. Then he continued, "It's never okay to bully others just because they are different. Imagine how you would feel if other fairies were bullying you."

"He's right," said a voice from the front of the classroom. They all looked at the voice and realized that the teacher already came in. When they saw her, the forest fairies flew to their seats in a hurry. Vincent knelt in front of the water fairy and stretched out his hand, "Come on, you don't have to worry now. You can sit with me."

She smiled at Vincent and took his hand. Vincent felt happy because he was able to stand up to bullies and teach them an important lesson.

Fighting and Making Up

Have you ever seen a yeti before? It's very difficult to see yetis as they live in the snowiest part of the world and they blend well with their surroundings. Even though yetis spend most of their days in the deep, dark caves in the mountains, the young ones love exploring, especially when there are blizzards.

"Come on, Craig!" Charles the yeti said.

Charles and Craig were best friends who made a promise to always meet in the giant rock when a blizzard came. From there, they would explore the different parts of the mountain together. Charles and Craig wanted to become expert explorers.

"I'm coming," Craig cried out. Charles was a lot bigger and stronger than Craig. Even though they were of the same age, their difference in size was clear as day. Charles was from one of the biggest yeti families while Craig was from one of the smallest. Since their families were very close, they grew up as best friends.

"You know I'm not as fast as you, Charles," Craig said.

"How can you become an expert explorer if you can't keep up?" Charles said with a laugh. Because of the blizzard, Charles didn't see that his words hurt Craig's feelings. He just kept running up the mountain so that he could reach the top. Once in a while, he would stop, call out to Craig, and wait for him to answer.

"Come on!" Charles called out again. He waited for a while but didn't get an answer. "Craig?" Charles said loudly. "Where are you?"

Still, his best friend didn't answer. Charles felt worried. His parents would be very upset if he lost Craig. He slowly climbed down the mountain to look for Craig. Because of the blizzard, Charles couldn't see well. He kept walking and calling out to Craig that he didn't see the big hole in the snow.

"Ah!" Charles cried out as he fell in the hole. When he looked up, he saw that he couldn't crawl out of the hole as it was too high.

"Uh-oh," Charles said, "how will I get out now?"

Charles tried to think of a way to crawl out when he heard footsteps above. He looked up and said, "Hey! Is someone up there?"

The sound of the footsteps stopped and after a moment, a small, furry head peeped into the hole, "Charles?"

Charles saw his best friend at the top of the hole. He smiled and said, "Craig! There you are! I'm so happy to see you!"

"Oh, yeah?" Craig said with a frown. "I thought I was just slowing you down."

Charles was surprised. Craig never talked to him like this before. When he looked at his best friend's face, he saw that Craig looked upset. Charles asked, "Are you mad at me?"

"What do you think?" Craig said. "You always say mean things to me just because I'm smaller than you."

"Oh," Charles said. He didn't realize that his jokes made his best friend feel bad. Now Charles felt bad too. He looked up and said, "I'm so sorry, Craig. Whenever I make jokes, I don't mean to hurt you. I'm just trying to be funny."

"Okay," Craig said, "just try to watch your words next time. You don't have to keep reminding me that I'm smaller than you."

"I promise," Charles said with a smile.

"Thanks," Craig said as he smiled back. "Now wait here," said Craig. A few moments later, he came back with a long, thick vine. He threw the vine into the hole and Charles used it to climb out.

"Thank you, Craig!" Charles said happily. Craig smiled at his best friend and they continued exploring the mountain together. This time, Charles minded his words so his best friend won't get upset anymore.

My Genie Friend

Charlotte the unicorn was fond of making wishes. Whenever she saw stars in the sky, she would make a wish. Right before she blew the candles out on her birthday, she would make a wish. Even when she found dandelions in the meadow, she would close her eyes, and make a wish first before blowing on them. To Charlotte, wishes made life wonderful!

One day, when Charlotte was walking home from the meadow, she saw something glittery inside a dark cave. Charlotte wondered what the glittery thing was but she was too scared to go inside the cave by herself, especially since the sun was already going down. She thought about going inside the cave to see what the shiny thing was but then, she had a bright idea. Tomorrow morning, she planned to come back here when it is bright and sunny. Charlotte took one last look inside the cave and headed home.

The next morning, Charlotte woke up feeling excited. She jumped out of bed and ran to the dining room to have breakfast. "Good morning, Charlotte," greeted her mom.

"Good morning, mom," Charlotte said. She sat down and started eating her breakfast in a rush. Charlotte's Mom looked at her in surprise and said, "Why are you eating so fast, Charlotte? Are you late for something?"

"Oh," Charlotte said, "no, I just need to go somewhere right after breakfast. Is that okay?"

"Alright," said her mom, "just be home before the sun goes down. It's not safe for young unicorns to stay out at night."

"Thank you, mom!" Charlotte said. She had already finished her breakfast and she was ready to go back to the cave. Charlotte gave her Mom a quick kiss and galloped out of the house. A few minutes later, she was back in front of the cave. She quickly ran inside the cave, picked up the shiny object with her mouth, and ran back out. When she dropped the shiny object, she saw that it was a lamp!

"Oh," said Charlotte, "I wonder if there is a genie inside this lamp." She rubbed the lamp with her hoof and smoke came out of it and along with the smoke was a genie!

"I'm free!" said the genie. Then he looked at Charlotte and said, "You're a unicorn!"

"Yes," Charlotte answered with a smile. "My name is Charlotte. What's your name?"

"I am the great Elijah," said the genie, "and for setting me free, I will grant you three wishes."

Since Charlotte loved making wishes, she knew exactly what she wanted. She said, "For my first wish, I wish for fruit trees to grow all over our house. That way, my Mom doesn't have to walk to the forest to gather fruit."

Elijah smiled at her and said, "That's a very nice wish. Now, I will grant it!"

"Thank you," Charlotte said with a smile. Then she continued, "For my second wish, I wish to always have magical adventures just like this one."

Elijah smiled again and said, "I love granting this wish! Adventures are super fun and now, I will grant your wish!"

"Thanks again!" Charlotte said. Elijah looked at Charlotte and said, "Are you ready to make your last wish?"

"Yes," Charlotte said. She knew exactly what she wanted to wish for. She looked up at Elijah and said, "I have always wanted to have a genie friend. For my last wish, I wish to set you free so you don't have to be trapped in your lamp forever."

Elijah's eyes grew big. He said, "Nobody has ever wished me free before. Are you sure that is what you want?"

"Yes!" Charlotte said. "As long as you promise to be my friend."

"Of course!" Elijah said as his lamp started fading away. "Thank you, Charlotte. I am so happy to have a kind and selfless friend like you." Since then, Charlotte and Elijah became close friends who went on many adventures together.

We Are All Different

Chapter 3:
We Are All Different

As children grow up, it's important for them to realize that we are all different and that's okay. At some point, your child will ask you questions about why some of their friends look different, talk differently, dress differently, and even act differently. The beauty of our world comes from the diversity of its people. Through these stories, you can teach your child all about learning how to accept differences instead of making fun of those who stand out.

The Odd One Out

"Come on, Martin," said the mother dragon, "it's time to get up."

Martin the dragon opened his eyes, looked out the window, and said, "Mom, the sun hasn't even risen yet."

"I know," answered Martin's mom, "but we have a long way to travel."

Today was a very special day for dragons. One day each year, all of the dragons gather on a secret island that no other creatures know about. Here, they meet other dragons and have a big celebration from morning until night. All dragons look forward to this celebration, especially those who are friends with dragons from different lands. But Martin never felt excited when this special day came. He always felt like he was the odd one out because he didn't have a dad.

Ever since he could remember, Martin's family was only made up of himself and his mom. When they flew all the way to the Island of Dragons, all the dragons his age had moms, dads, brothers, and sisters. Because of this, Martin always hid in the trees and waited for the celebrations to be over so that his Mom can take him home.

"Do we have to go, mom?" Martin asked as he stretched his legs, wings, and tail.

"You know the answer to that, Martin," his Mom answered with a smile on her face. "You ask me that same question every year. And as I said, if you tried talking to the other young dragons, you might have more fun." Martin sighed and stood up. He stretched his wings and went to look for food while his Mom prepared for the trip.

After Martin finished his breakfast, his Mom called his name again. "I'm coming, mom," Martin answered. Then he went outside and saw his Mom waiting for him with a big smile on her face. Martin smiled back at his mom. Then they both stretched their wings and flew into the sky.

It took about half an hour for Martin and his Mom to reach the mysterious Island of Dragons. When they landed, Martin's Mom immediately saw some of her friends. She waved at them and looked at her son, "This year, try to talk to the other young dragons, okay?"

"I'll think about it, mom," Martin said as he watched his Mom join her friends. When Martin was left alone, he turned around and headed towards the trees. Just then, a voice behind him said, "So, you're going to hide in the trees all day again?"

Martin stopped, turned his head, and saw a young dragon behind him. She was a bit smaller than him and she had a warm smile on her face. "I-I was just going to sit down in the shade for a while," Martin said. He was feeling very shy because this was the first time he had ever talked to another young dragon.

"My name is Beth," the young dragon said. She walked up to Martin and continued, "Your name is Martin, right? I see you and your Mom arrive every year but then you disappear right away!"

"I don't like this event much," Martin said.

"Why?" Beth asked.

"I always feel out of place," Martin replied feeling embarrassed. "All of the dragon families here are complete but mine isn't. It's just me and my mom."

"Is that all?" Beth asked. Then her smile turned sad as she said, "My family isn't complete either. It's just me, my dad, and my little sister. We lost our Mom a few years ago."

"Really?" Martin asked as his eyes grew wide.

"Yes," Beth said, "and celebrating with the other young dragons always makes me feel better. So, do you want to hang out with me and the others this year?"

Martin smiled at Beth. Suddenly, he didn't feel so alone anymore. He decided that this year, he was going to celebrate and have fun with the other young dragons.

Making Fun of Others Is No Fun at All

Dianne the troll was always daydreaming in class. She had a creative mind and a lot of imaginative ideas. When she came into class, she would listen to her teacher for a few minutes before her mind would start wandering to other things. Dianne thought about going on great adventures while she explored the different parts of the world. Since she was still young, Dianne wasn't allowed to explore by herself. So she used her imagination to break free and visit faraway places.

One day, while Dianne was imagining herself flying with fairies, she didn't realize that her teacher was calling her name.

"Dianne!" her teacher said as the little troll snapped out of her daydream.

"Y-yes?" she said while feeling surprised. When she looked around, she saw all of her friends staring at her and snickering. She could feel herself blushing as she stood up.

"I have called your name five times already, Dianne," her teacher said.

"I'm sorry," Dianne answered.

"Your daydreaming will get you into a lot of trouble one of these days," Dianne's teacher said and this made her classmates laugh out loud.

"Okay, that's enough," said the teacher angrily. Then she looked at Dianne and said, "Please come forward and answer the question on the blackboard."

Even though her classmates weren't laughing anymore, Dianne still felt ashamed. She walked to the front of the class and answered the question. It's a good thing she knew the answer or her classmates might laugh at her again.

When Dianne was done, she went back to her seat and this time, she tried not to daydream.

After a few hours of listening to her teacher, the recess bell rang. Dianne stood up immediately and ran outside before any of her classmates. She found a shaded spot in the playground, sat down, and started eating her snack. Moments later, a group of troll girls walked towards Dianne.

"Hi, daydreamer," said the meanest troll girl of the group. "What were you dreaming about?"

"Nothing," Dianne said. She looked down and continued eating.

"You know what," the troll girl continued, "you're the weirdest troll in our class. That's why you don't have any friends!" Then all the other troll girls laughed. Dianne almost cried when she heard a voice that said, "Hey!"

Trina, another troll girl in their class, ran up to the group of girls and stood in front of them bravely. She said, "Don't you have anything better to do?"

The mean troll girl looked at Trina angrily and said, "Who are you, her protector?"

"I'm her friend," Trina said even though she wasn't very close to Dianne. Then she continued, "It's not nice to make fun of others. You might think it makes you cool but the truth is, it just makes you a mean person."

Dianne looked up at Trina. She couldn't believe how brave this young troll was. Trina was even smaller than any of the girls in the group. The other troll girls looked embarrassed but their leader just gave Trina a mean smile. Then she said, "Come on, girls. This isn't fun anymore."

As the group of troll girls walked away, Dianne said, "Thank you."

Trina turned around and smiled at Dianne. She sat down next to the daydreaming troll and said, "Don't mind them. They just want to make others feel bad so that they can feel better about themselves. Are you okay?"

"Yes," Dianne said with a smile.

"Don't be afraid to stand up to trolls like them. When they see that you're brave and you will stand up for what is right, they will leave you alone," Trina explained.

"Thanks," Dianne said again, "I will remember that." Then Dianne and Trina swapped stories as they shared their snacks with each other.

The Unicorn With No Horn

All unicorns take great pride in their horns. Some horns are silver, some are gold, and some have all the colors of the rainbow. When unicorns reach a certain age, their horns start growing and when this happens, they can start taking flying lessons too.

Every morning, Riley the unicorn woke up feeling excited. This was the year when his horn would start growing. Whenever he woke up, he would run to the mirror and check his forehead. All of Riley's friends were preparing to take flying lessons in the summer as their horns had already popped out of their foreheads.

This morning, Riley opened his eyes, jumped out of bed, and ran to the mirror as he always did. But when he saw his reflection, he didn't see anything on his forehead. Riley felt disappointed. Summer was only a few weeks away and he might not be able to join this year's flying lessons.

"Good morning, Mom and Dad," Riley said sadly as he entered the dining room.

"Good morning, Riley," said his mom.

"Hi, son," said his dad, "why the long face?"

Riley went to his place at the dining table and said, "No horn yet." Then he started eating his food. He was too sad to notice that his parents exchanged smiles while he ate.

After breakfast, Riley went out to meet his friends. When he saw them, he felt bad again as he saw that their horns were growing bigger and bigger. "Hey, guys," Riley said as he put on a brave smile for his friends.

"Hi Riley!" his friends said one by one. None of them asked him about his horn because they knew that he was feeling bad about it. This was one thing that Riley loved about his group of friends. They were always supportive of one another no matter what happens. His best friend even said that if Riley's horn didn't come out by the summer, he didn't mind taking lessons with Riley on the next summer break.

Riley and his friends spent the whole day together. They played in the fields, picked apples from the forest and enjoyed them as a snack, and sat around in a circle in Flyer's Peak. This was where all young unicorns learned how to fly. Every summer, the flying instructor would teach young unicorns to fly and for their final test, the young unicorns would take off from Flyer's Peak.

While his friends sat in a circle, Riley stood up and walked towards the edge of the cliff. He stood there and tried to imagine how it would feel if it was his time to soar. Just then, his best friend Avery walked up to him and said, "Hey, what are you thinking about?"

"Nothing," Riley said with a smile. "But I need to go home now. I'll see you again tomorrow."

Riley said goodbye to the rest of his friends and went home. When he walked into his house, he saw his parents standing with the flying instructor!

"Oh, hi," Riley said.

Riley's parents smiled at him and his Mom said, "Hi, Riley. Please, sit down."

"This is Riley," his Dad said to the flying instructor, "and this is Mr. Burton."

"I know," Riley said shyly, "I was looking forward to taking flying lessons with Mr. Burton this summer."

"Well," Mr. Burton said, "that's great because your parents just signed you up for flying lessons this summer!"

"What?" Riley said. "But I don't have my horn yet."

Riley's Dad walked over to him and said, "That's okay, Riley because you're a very special unicorn. Once every ten years, unicorns without horns are born in every unicorn village. In our village, you are that unicorn, Riley. That makes you very special."

Then Riley's Mom said, "It also means that you can join your friends this summer to take your flying lessons."

"It's an honor to teach you, Riley," said Mr. Burton. "I have never taught a hornless unicorn before."

Riley smiled at Mr. Burton and said, "I can't wait!"

We Can All Be Friends

The best school in the land of magical creatures was the one that welcomed all types of creatures to come and study together. Other schools only allowed one type of magical creature to enroll, like the School of Unicorns, the School of Trolls, and the School of Dragons. But in Magic Academy, all creatures big and small were welcome.

Monica was one of the centaurs who studied at Magic Academy. She loved her school because she loved meeting all kinds of creatures. Monica was a very friendly young centaur and because of her kind heart, all the other students chose her to be the president of the student council. Monica took this job seriously. Whenever another student was in trouble, she was there to help out.

"Monica," called out one of the students, "Principal Hawke wants to see you."

"Oh," said Monica, "thanks for telling me. Now go to class before the bell rings so you won't be late."

She looked at the clock and saw that she only had ten minutes before the bell rang. She had to hurry so she galloped all the way to the Principal's office. When she got there, she knocked on the door.

"Come in," came Principal Hawke's voice from inside the office. Monica opened the door, went inside, and said, "Good morning, Principal Hawke. Did you want to see me?"

"Yes," said the principal with a smile. "I wanted to talk to you about a new student who just enrolled in the school. Her name is Raven and she is a griffin. Her mother came in yesterday and enrolled her. But she also said that Raven isn't very friendly because she was bullied in her previous school."

"Oh," said Monica, "that's so sad. Bullying is never good."

"I know," said Principal Hawke. "I am very proud of our school because none of the students bully others even though we have different creatures here. Raven came from the exclusive School of Griffins but she was never happy there."

"I will make her feel welcome here," Monica promised.

Principal Hawke smiled at the centaur and said, "I know you will. Raven's mother has to take care of some chores this morning so she will only bring Raven to school after recess. I will send her to your class right away."

"Okay," Monica said, "for now, I need to go to class. The bell is about to ring. I will wait for her to come. Thank you, Principal Hawke."

"Thank you too, Monica. Have a great day in class," answered the principal.

Monica went back to class and talked to her classmates about the new student. She told them about how Raven was bullied at her previous school and this made them upset. In Magic Academy, all students learned to accept others no matter how different they were. Bullying didn't exist in their school and this was why all of the students in Magic Academy were happy.

After recess, Principal Hawke knocked on the door of Monica's classroom. When Monica's teacher opened the door, Monica saw a small griffin with the principal.

"Hello, everyone. This is Raven and she will be your new classmate," the principal announced.

Monica walked towards Raven and gave her a big smile. She said, "Hi, Raven! My name is Monica and I am the president of the school council."

Raven gave Monica a small smile and said, "Hi," in a very soft voice.

"You can sit with Monica, Raven," said the teacher. So Monica and Raven sat together. Then Monica said to their new classmate, "Don't worry, Raven. Our class might look different from what you are used to. But we all believe that we can be friends despite our differences."

This warm explanation made Raven smile. Somehow, she knew that she would be happy at the Magic Academy.

Learning How To Be Brave

Chapter 4:
Learning How To Be Brave

As children grow up, they will have to face situations that might seem like little things to adults but are terrifying for children. Although you would like to protect your child from these kinds of situations, you also want them to learn how to be brave. This is the theme of the stories in this chapter. Hopefully, your child will be inspired by these stories so they can find their inner courage when faced with scary situations.

No Doctors, Please!

Anthony is one of the elves who live in the Land of Elves. He was a young, adventurous elf who spent a lot of time outdoors. Anthony loved how the sun felt on his skin, how the breeze blew his hair, and how the rain felt as drops fell onto his head. But Anthony's Dad always reminded him to find shade when it was raining.

Young elves shouldn't get wet in the rain because it will make them sick. When young elves get sick, they have to visit the elf doctor who lives in the deepest, darkest part of the Land of the Elves. One day, Anthony planned to spend time on the hill of sunflowers. The smell of sunflowers was very comforting to him so he would go to this hill one time every month.

"Dad, I'm going to the hill of sunflowers," Anthony said.

"Okay," Anthony's Dad said from the kitchen, "just remember to find a shaded place if it starts raining."

"Alright, Dad. See you later," Anthony called out. Then he walked out the door to visit his favorite place in the Land of Elves. When he reached the hill, Anthony smiled. He really loved this place. Anthony sat down on top of one of the rocks and stared at the sky, he closed his eyes and felt the wind in his face. Then Anthony lay down on the rock to watch the clouds. After a few moments, Anthony didn't realize that he fell asleep. While he was sleeping, Anthony didn't see that rain clouds gathered in the sky. It got darker and darker until heavy rain poured down.

When Anthony woke up, he was already soaking wet! "Oh, no," he said as he stood up. He hopped off the rock and tried to look for a shady spot to hide under until the rain stops. But since he was on a hill, there wasn't anything tall enough to shade him from the rain. So Anthony decided to run all the way home.

When he went inside his house, Anthony's Dad saw that he was drenched. "Anthony!" his Dad called out. "You're soaked! Dry off quickly or you might get sick," he said as he handed a towel and some dry clothes to the young elf.

But even if Anthony dried off when he got home, she still got sick the next morning. His Dad woke him up early in the morning with a cup of tea in his hands, "Wake up, Anthony. We have to go to the doctor."

"No!" Anthony cried out. Just like all other young elves, Anthony was terrified of going to the doctor. He didn't want to go to the deepest, darkest part of the Land of the Elves and he didn't want to see the doctor.

"I'm fine, Dad," Anthony said, "I don't even feel sick."

Anthony's Dad stood up and took a small mirror. He gave the mirror to Anthony and said, "You're burning up and you have spots all over your face. You need to visit the doctor." Anthony took the mirror and looked at his reflection. His Dad was right! He had so many spots all over his face and when he touched his cheeks, they were very hot.

"But, Dad," Anthony said, "I'm scared."

Anthony's Dad smiled at him and said, "I know you are. But the doctor is the only person who can make you feel better. He might seem like someone scary but just like all other doctors, he just wants what's best for you."

"O-okay, Dad," Anthony said. "I will be brave so that I can get better." Then he smiled at his Dad as they started preparing to go to the doctor.

Helping Others Out

The sea monster families in the sea usually stay inside their homes. Since the population of humans on land grew, the sea monsters didn't like going up to the surface. They were afraid of humans because humans always tried to catch them with their nets and sharp spears.

Rachel was a young sea monster who grew up sharing her parents' fear of humans. She spent all of her time with her Mom, Dad, and her two younger sisters. Rachel had never met other young sea monsters before but she knew that they were out there.

"Mom," have you ever met another sea monster before?" Rachel asked her Mom while they were having dinner one day.

Rachel's whole family stopped eating and they looked at her with wide eyes. "Why would you ask me that, Rachel?" her Mom asked.

"Oh, it's nothing," Rachel replied. She wanted to learn more about other sea monsters but she also knew that her parents didn't like talking about the world outside of their home. When she continued eating, her parents gave her one last look then they continued their meals too.

After dinner, Rachel and her family spent some time sharing stories in the living room. They did this every night before going to bed. While Rachel's sisters were always excited to hear the stories shared by their parents, she wasn't. Ever since she could remember, Rachel listened to those stories. By now, she had already memorized most of them. After storytime, Rachel and her sisters said goodnight to their parents and to each other. Then they swam to their rooms to go to sleep.

That night, Rachel couldn't sleep in her bed. She kept remembering how her parents looked when she asked about other sea monsters. Rachel knew that humans were dangerous but were the other sea monsters dangerous too? While she lay down in her bed thinking, she heard a sound from outside.

Rachel sat up and listened. The sound came again, "Help!"

She immediately swam up to her window and looked out into the darkness. "Help!" came the sound again.

Rachel swam to the door of her bedroom and opened it. She peeked outside and saw that her parent's bedroom door was already closed. Quietly, she swam all the way to their front door and opened it. Although she was feeling a bit scared, Rachel wanted to help the creature who was calling out.

She listened again and when she heard the call, she swam towards the sound. Moments later, she could hear the call coming from a forest of seaweed, "Help me!"

"Hello?" Rachel called out.

"Is someone out there? Please help me, I'm trapped!" the voice called out.

Rachel slithered through the seaweed and saw a young sea monster tangled near the bottom. She helped the young sea monster out of the seaweed and they both swam out together.

"Thank you!" said the young sea monster.

"You're welcome. My name is Rachel, what's yours?" Rachel said.

"My name is Arianna," answered the young sea monster. "I was exploring when I swam right into the seaweed forest and got trapped. It's a good thing a brave sea monster like you helped me."

Rachel smiled, "It's already late and it's very dark. We should go home. I hope to see you again soon."

"You too," said Arianna, "thanks again." Then the two young sea monsters swam back to their homes feeling happy.

Performing on Stage

Lorem "I can't wait to perform in the talent show!" Genevieve said excitedly. She was swimming with her brother Jeff. They came from school, where their teacher just announced that there was going to be a talent show next week. Although Genevieve felt happy and excited about it, Jeff was feeling scared.

Jeff and Genevieve were twins. Just like their mom, they had beautiful singing voices and when they sang together, everyone who listened was amazed at how lovely their voices blended together. Genevieve loved to sing in front of friends, family, and anyone else who wanted to listen to her. But Jeff wasn't like his twin sister at all. He only sang in front of his family as he was too shy to sing in front of other people.

"What are we going to sing, Jeff?" Genevieve asked when they got home.

"What?" Jeff asked his sister with a shocked expression on his face.

"What are we going to sing for the talent show?" Genevieve asked again.

Jeff shook his head and said, "I don't know what you're going to sing but I won't be joining you."

Genevieve's eyes grew wide. She looked at her brother to see if he was joking. Then she said, "You can't do that to me, Jeff. You have to sing with me! When we sing together, everyone loves it!"

Jeff answered, "You know I don't like performing in front of other people, Genevieve. Just join the talent show without me."

"But you're my twin! We should support each other!" Genevieve answered back. Tears were forming in her eyes as she realized that her brother was serious. When Josh didn't answer her, Genevieve swam away while crying.

When Josh was alone, he started feeling bad. He didn't like making his sister cry but he was too afraid to perform. The thought of standing on a stage and singing in front of the whole school made him feel sick. While he was lost in his thoughts, Jeff didn't realize that his Mom arrived.

"Hey, Jeff. Are you okay?" his Mom asked. She sat beside the young mermaid.

"Not really," Jeff answered. "I feel bad because I made Genevieve cry."

"Oh," said his mom, "why did you make her cry?"

"I didn't mean to mom," Jeff said defensively. "Today, our teacher announced that there was going to be a talent show. Genevieve wanted us to sing together but I don't want to."

"Why not, Jeff? You have a beautiful voice!" his Mom said.

"I'm... scared," Jeff admitted.

Jeff's Mom looked at him and gave him a warm smile, "You were always so shy, Jeff. But you know what?"

Jeff looked up and said, "What?"

"We all believe in you," his Mom said. "Just like Genevieve, you have a beautiful talent to share with the world. If you can find the courage to step on that stage and share your talent, we will all support you."

"Okay," Jeff said. After a moment, he stood up and said, "I have to go, mom. I need to look for Genevieve so that we can start practicing for the talent show."

Jeff's Mom smiled and nodded. She felt proud of her son. She knew how shy Jeff was but he agreed to perform. Jeff's Mom was happy because her son had finally chosen to be brave.

Monsters in the Dark

Centaurs lived in the forest in tribes. Each tribe lived in a different part of the forest and they got along well with all the other magical creatures. By nature, centaurs are very peaceful and fun-loving. When problems arise, their elders would come together to talk until they reach a solution. Another thing that centaurs were famous for was being very brave. If needed, centaurs would face the scariest enemies just to protect their families and the rest of their tribe.

Naomi was a young centaur who had all the traits of her kind. But when the sun goes down and the forest becomes dark, Naomi becomes scared. All the other centaurs of her tribe aren't bothered by the darkness. But Naomi is terrified of the forest when night time comes because she believes that monsters are hiding in the shadows.

"Mom, can you sleep with me tonight?" Naomi asked.

"Oh, Naomi," said her mom, "you know that young centaurs have to sleep alone. Remember that being a centaur means being brave."

"I know, mom. But just this once, can you please sleep with me?" Naomi begged her mom.

Naomi's Mom chuckled softly, "You ask me that every night, Naomi. And every morning, you wake up and realize that you slept through the night on your own. You are braver than you think, my dear."

"Okay," Naomi said, "goodnight mom."

"Goodnight, Naomi," her mother said as she kissed the young centaur on her forehead.

When Naomi's Mom left, Naomi lay in her bed with her eyes wide open. She didn't like being left alone in her room at night. Just as she was about to fall asleep, she heard soft footsteps in the darkness. Naomi sat up and whispered, "H-hello?"

She heard the footsteps running towards the corner of her room. Then the footsteps stopped. Naomi stood up from her bed and said, "Is someone there?" She carefully walked to the other end of her room and picked up a lamp filled with glow worms. She shook the lamp to wake the worms up and when they did, they started to glow. Naomi took a deep breath, turned around, and looked at the corner of the room where she heard the footsteps.

She saw a small, furry monster hiding in the corner of her room. The monster was covering its eyes and it was shaking all over. This time, instead of feeling scared, she felt sorry for the little monster. She walked towards the monster and knelt down. Then she said, "Hello, my name is Naomi."

The monster looked up at Naomi and said, "H-hi."

Naomi smiled at the monster, "Don't be afraid, I won't hurt you."

The little monster stopped shaking. Then it stood up and said, "My name is Bailey. I'm sorry if I scared you. I came into the wrong house."

Naomi giggled which made Bailey the monster smile. "I was so scared that a monster was in my room. But now that I see you, I'm not scared anymore!"

"That's good," said Bailey, "you don't have to be scared of me. You're a centaur! One of the bravest creatures in the forest."

"I hope we can be friends," Naomi said.

"I would love that!" answered Bailey. "I can't wait to tell the other monsters that I have a centaur friend and a very brave one at that."

Naomi smiled at her new friend. Suddenly, the darkness didn't seem too scary anymore.

Respecting Our Elders

Chapter 5:
Respecting Our Elders

No matter what age your child is, it's important for them to learn how to respect all of their elders. Respect is one of the most fundamental values that children must learn. As your child grows up, they will also earn respect because of how they treat others. In this chapter, you can explain this abstract concept through stories about magical creatures. This will help your child understand what it truly means to show respect.

Breaking the Rules

Bonnie was one of the most mischievous witches in the village. She was very smart, she loved to learn, and she had a natural talent for magic. But most of the witch elders in the village didn't like talking to Bonnie because she never listened to anyone, not even to her parents.

One day, all of the witch elders gathered in the magical castle to have a meeting. Since Bonnie's Mom was one of the witch elders, she was able to tag along. Bonnie was very excited as she had never been inside the magical castle before.

"Remember, Bonnie," her Mom warned, "you should only stay in the room I will place you in."

"But mom, I want to explore the magical castle!" Bonnie argued.

"You're too young for that, Bonnie," her Mom said. "I brought you along so that you can see the magical castle. But one thing you must remember is that you should follow the rules."

"Fine," Bonnie said but in her mind, she knew that she would explore the magical castle on her own. When Bonnie and her Mom arrived, the door of the magical castle opened on its own. Bonnie and her Mom went inside but Bonnie didn't see anyone else. "Where is everybody, mom?" Bonnie asked.

"They are already in the meeting room," Bonnie's Mom said. "They are waiting for me." She led Bonnie into a room with a black door. Again, the door opened on its own, and Bonnie saw that inside, the room was very colorful. Bonnie's Mom pulled her into the room and said, "This room is for young witches like you. Promise me that you will only stay in this room and wait for me to come back."

Bonnie looked at her Mom and nodded. Her Mom gave her a quick hug, left the room, and closed the door. When Bonnie was alone in the room, she looked around. "Everything is so childish here," Bonnie said. Because she was so smart, Bonnie believed that she was old enough to explore the magical castle. She opened the door and stepped out into the hallway.

Bonnie looked around but didn't see anyone. Then she smiled and started exploring. As Bonnie walked through the hallway, she didn't see anything interesting. When they reached the end of the hallway, she met a very old witch.

"Oh!" said Bonnie.

The witch looked at her and said, "What is a young witch like you doing here?"

"My Mom brought me along with her. She joined the meeting of elders and she said that I could explore," Bonnie explained.

The old witch said, "That's not true. If your mother is one of the elders, she would have left you in the room for young witches. You are breaking the rules, young lady."

"That room is boring!" Bonnie exclaimed. "I just want to explore the magical castle. You're not my Mom so I don't have to listen to you!"

"Very well," said the old witch. Then she walked away. Bonnie watched the old witch leave. Then she smiled and went back to exploring. But then, Bonnie realized that she couldn't move! She tried calling for help but she couldn't talk either! Because Bonnie broke her promise and didn't show respect to her elders, she was now frozen in place. For hours, Bonnie stayed in the corner of the hallway.

Then when it was almost night time, she heard footsteps running towards her. Bonnie felt someone hugging her and suddenly, she could move again! When she looked up, she saw her mom, "I'm so sorry, mom!" Bonnie said as she started crying.

Bonnie's Mom knelt down and looked at her in the eye, "You broke your promise."

"I know," Bonnie said, "and I was very rude too. I'm so sorry."

Bonnie's Mom smiled at her and said, "It looks like you have learned your lesson."

"Yes," Bonnie said, "I promise not to break the rules. I also promise to be more respectful, especially to my elders." This time, Bonnie meant every word she said.

Getting Into Trouble

Most giants are gentle and they like to stay in their villages so they don't scare the other creatures. But in one of the Giant Villages, there was this one young giant named Oscar who never listened to his elders. He enjoyed leaving the village to scare the other creatures, especially the fairies in the swamp. One of Oscar's favorite pastimes was to go into the swamp and hide behind the big rocks. Then when fairies would land on the rocks, he would jump up and scare them. Oscar would laugh out loud whenever the fairies would fall into the swamp from the shock.

One day, Oscar planned to go into the swamp again. He quickly ate his breakfast and said goodbye to his parents. He told them that he was just going to the park to play with the other young giants. But he was planning something more mischievous. When he stepped out of the door, he saw his grandfather standing in the street. Oscar didn't like his grandfather very much. His grandfather was very strict.

"Good morning, Oscar," his grandfather said in a deep and loud voice.

"Good morning, grandfather," Oscar replied. He was about to wave goodbye to his grandfather when the old giant asked him, "Where are you off to, Oscar?"

"Oh," Oscar said, "I was on my way to the park to play with my friends."

"Is that so?" his grandfather asked again. Then the old giant knelt down in front of Oscar and placed his hands on the young giant's shoulders, "I wanted to talk to you about something."

"O-okay, grandfather," Oscar said, "what do you want to talk about?"

"The queen of the swamp fairies came to me this morning. She told me about a mischievous young giant who keeps hiding behind rocks to scare the swamp fairies," Oscar's grandfather explained.

"What has that got to do with me?" Oscar asked as he tried to look innocent.

"If that was you or any of your friends, you should stop. When fairies fall into the swamp, it takes hours for their wings to dry up. And when their wings are wet, they cannot fly," his grandfather continued.

"Okay," Oscar said, "I will tell my friends." He felt very bad about lying to his grandfather but he was too scared to admit that he was the one who kept scaring the swamp fairies.

"Alright then," Oscar's grandfather said. Then he stood up and went inside their house. Oscar breathed a sigh of relief then he continued walking towards the swamp. He still planned to scare the swamp fairies. "One last time," he said to himself.

When Oscar reached the swamp, he immediately hid behind the big rocks. A few moments later, he heard a pair of fairies land on the biggest rock. He smiled at the thought of scaring them. Oscar counted to ten in his mind, he jumped up, and gave a great big roar!

"Ah!" said the fairies. One of them flew up while the other one fell into the swamp. Again, this made Oscar laugh out loud. But he immediately stopped laughing when the other fairy flew right into his face and started screaming at him, "Why would you do that? Don't you have any respect for others?"

Then the fairy flew to the swamp to help the one who fell in. He said, "Let me help you out, my queen."

"Queen?" Oscar said. His eyes grew wide as he saw the fairy trying to pull the other fairy from the swamp. She was wearing a golden gown and a shiny crown on her head. Right away, Oscar knelt down and picked up the queen fairy gently. He placed her back on top of the rock then he said, "I'm so sorry, your majesty."

The queen looked up at Oscar and said, "I already spoke to your grandfather and yet, here you are again."

"I know," Oscar said, "please don't be mad at my grandfather. He talked to me this morning but I didn't listen."

"Please stop scaring us," the queen pleaded. "Even if you are big and we are small, you must learn how to respect all creatures."

"Yes, I understand now," Oscar said. "I promise not to do this again."

The queen looked at Oscar and smiled, "Alright, as long as you keep your promise."

Oscar smiled back. Then he took a leaf and used it to fan the queen until her wings were dry. Then Oscar left the swamp and never went back to scare the fairies again.

Why Should I Listen?

In the highest mountains where snow falls everyday live tribes of yetis. These yetis are huge and they are covered in white fur to keep them warm in the snow. Sarah was a young yeti who had never been outside of the cave before.

While yetis are still young, they must stay inside the cave because yetis only come out when there are strong blizzards. The snow from the blizzards keeps the yetis hidden making it the perfect kind of weather for them.

When young yetis reach five years of age, they can go outside with their parents to explore the mountains. As they grow older, they can start exploring the mountains on their own. Sarah was only four years old and she needed to wait for almost half a year before she could see the outside world.

"There you are, Sarah," said her mother as she sat down next to the young yeti.

Sarah looked up and smiled at her mom, "Hello, mom."

Sarah's Mom sat down next to her and looked outside. Snow was pouring in the mountains and young yetis had gone exploring. Sarah's Mom knew how much her daughter wanted to explore the world. Whenever she couldn't find her daughter, she would usually find the little yeti sitting here, at the entrance of their cave.

"Why can't I go outside, mom?" Sarah asked for the hundredth time.

"You know the answer to that, my dear." Her Mom replied. "Young yetis like you should stay inside the cave and you should always listen to your elders."

"Why should I listen, mom?" Sarah asked again.

"Because just like me, all the other elders want the young yetis to be safe," her Mom explained.

"But can't I just take a few steps outside? I want to feel the snow under my feet, in my face, and in my fur," Sarah argued.

Sarah's Mom gave her daughter a hug and said, "You only have a few months to go, Sarah. You've waited this long. I'm sure that you can wait a few months more." Then she stood up and went back inside the cave leaving Sarah sitting by herself.

As Sarah sat and waited for the other young yetis to come back, she kept thinking about what her Mom said. The elders wanted the young yetis to be safe but Sarah already knew how to take care of herself outside. Sarah stood up and looked around. There was nobody else around. She looked outside again and whispered to herself, "I'll just take a short walk and come back."

Sara stepped out into the blizzard. It felt wonderful! She could feel the snow on her feet, her fur, and her face. Sarah closed her eyes and took a deep breath. But then, a strong gust of wind blew and it took her along with it!

"Aaaaaah!" Sarah screamed as she flew into the air. "Help me!"

All she could see was white. The blizzard grew stronger and Sarah flew higher and higher into the air. She didn't know what to do. She didn't know how she would go back home. Sarah felt hopeless until something wrapped around her leg. Then she could feel herself being pulled back down to the ground. When Sarah looked down, she saw the other young yetis pulling her down.

"Almost!" called out one of the yetis. Then they stretched their arms out and grabbed onto Sarah. Once they got her, the young yetis ran into the cave and put Sarah down. "Are you okay?" one of them said.

"Y-yes," Sarah answered.

"Why did you go out, Sarah? You know that young yetis aren't allowed to go outside," said another.

"I-I know," Sarah said, "I'm sorry."

"Our elders know what's best for us and this is why we should listen to them," said one of the young yetis.

Sarah nodded and said, "Now I understand. I promise to listen to our elders so that I will always be safe. Thank you." The young yetis smiled at Sarah and gave her a hug to warm her up.

We Should Always Show Respect

To the centaurs, respect is a very important thing. While they are still young, centaurs learn how to respect their elders, their friends, and all of the creatures in the world. This was one thing that Frank the centaur knew by heart. But deep down, he didn't understand why respect is important. While he was spending a quiet afternoon with his family, Frank asked his parents, "Mom, Dad, why should we always show respect?"

Frank's parents looked up at him. His younger sister Francine looked at him too. Then Francine looked at her parents and said, "Yes, why is that so important?"

"Before we talk about the importance of respect, do either of you know what this word means?" their Dad asked.

Frank and Francine shook their heads. Then Frank said, "You and Mom always tell us to show respect. This is also what our teachers tell us at school all the time. But for some time now, I keep thinking... why is it important?"

"Respect is a feeling you have when you admire something or someone deeply because of the qualities, abilities or achievements they have. It is also something you give in regard for other creatures' traditions, rights, wishes or feelings," Frank's Dad explained.

"Okay," Frank said, "but if I don't admire someone, why should I show them respect?"

"What do you mean, Frank?" his Mom asked.

"Let me give you an example," Frank said as he tried to think of why he had this thought in the first place. "There is an old centaur at school. He is one of our teachers but nobody likes him. He's not very friendly and his classes are so boring! Even if he is like that, should I show respect to him?"

"Of course!" Frank's Mom said. "It is especially important to show him respect because he is older than you."

"But, why, mom?" Frank asked.

"Let me give you an example," Frank's Dad said. "Try to imagine how you would feel if you grew up to become a teacher and your students were all rude to you. None of them would listen to you and they even make fun of you because they think that your class is boring. How would you feel?"

Frank thought about the example his Dad shared. Then he said, "Well, I would feel bad."

"Of course you would," his Dad said with a smile. "Think about how much time and effort you would spend to learn how to become a teacher. Then after all that, your students won't show you any respect. It would be like all of your hard work was for nothing."

"You have a point," Frank told his dad.

"That is just one example and it only shows how you should respect your elders," Frank's Mom continued. "But the truth is, you should respect all creatures no matter how old, young or different they are. When we all learn how to respect each other, the world becomes a happier and more peaceful place."

"That's wonderful, mom!" Francine said. "Doesn't that sound wonderful, Frank? If everyone got along because we all showed respect to each other?"

Frank smiled at his sister. He now understood the true importance of respect. He said, "Yes, Francine. Showing respect will surely make us better centaurs too."

Exploring The World

Chapter 6:
Exploring The World

The world is a beautiful place and for children, the possibilities are endless. If your child loves to explore, the stories in this chapter will surely fill them with joy and wonder. Since the world of these characters is very different from ours, the imagination of your child will soar as you share these stories with them.

Beauties and the Beasts

Paula and Olive were mermaid sisters who explored all over their kingdom. While they enjoyed spending time with their friends when they weren't in school, they enjoyed exploring with each other more. Even though they looked nothing alike, these two sisters were very close. Olive had a dark green tail and silver hair just like their Dad and their younger brother while Paula had a bright orange tail and golden hair just like their mom. Sometimes, when they were swimming together, other creatures thought that they were best friends.

"Where do you want to go today, Olive?" Paula said. Paula was the older sister. Olive thought about her sister's question for a moment before she answered, "Can we go to the caves?"

"Which caves?" asked Paula.

"How about the spooky ones at the edge of our kingdom?" Olive said with excitement. Even though she was younger, Olive was much braver than Paula. Unlike her older sister, Olive wasn't afraid to explore even the darkest caves.

"Does it have to be those caves?" Paula asked.

"Come on, Paula. You asked me where I wanted to go!" Olive answered.

"Fine," Paula said.

The two sisters swam towards the edge of the kingdom to explore the caves. It was quite far since their kingdom was very big. When they reached the caves, the sisters were out of breath. They sat on some rocks at the entrance of the cave to rest. While resting, they heard a strange noise coming from the cave.

"What was that?" Olive asked excitedly.

"I-I don't know," Paula said worriedly.

"Let's go inside to see what made that noise, Paula," Olive said as she swam up to the dark entrance of the cave.

"What?" Paula asked her sister. "It might have been something dangerous! I say we go home."

The two sisters started arguing about whether or not they should go inside the cave. Paula was worried that something might happen to them. Since she was older, Paula knew that she would get into trouble if either of them got hurt. Olive just wanted to find out what was making the noise inside the cave. As the sisters argued with each other, a sea monster swam out of the cave yelling, "Help!"

"Oh!" the sisters cried out together. The sea monster stopped right in front of the girls then said, "Thank goodness! Please help me!"

The two sisters looked at each other then nodded. They knew that they should help. The sea monster swam back inside the cave followed by Paula and Olive. As soon as the sea monster swam inside, the scales at the back of his body started glowing. Suddenly, it wasn't dark anymore.

When Paula, Olive, and the sea monster reached a deep part of the cave, the two sisters saw another sea monster who was trapped under a heavy rock. "Carl!" the sea monster said. "I found these two mermaids, they can help me lift the rock."

Together, they pulled hard until they lifted the rock just enough for Carl the sea monster to slither out. "Thank you!" he said. The two sea monsters gave each other a high five then they looked at the mermaids. Carl said, "It's nice to meet you. My name is Carl and this is my brother, Harry. Thank you for helping me."

"You're welcome," Olive said with a smile.

"My name is Paula and this is my sister, Olive," Paula said.

"Do your scales glow because of magic?" Olive asked.

The two sea monsters chuckled then Harry said, "No, our scales just glow naturally when we go into dark places. It helps us see in the dark."

"That's amazing!" Olive cried out. "Can you explore these dark caves with us? The light from your scales will make exploring a lot easier."

"Sure!" said the brothers. Then the mermaid sisters and sea monster brother explored the rest of the cave together. Since then, they have become great friends.

Land and Air

Victoria was a tiny elf who lived with her family in the village of elves. Small as she was, Victoria was one of the bravest elves in the village. Aside from being very brave, Victoria was also very friendly. This allowed her to make friends with different kinds of creatures, not just elves.

One day, while Victoria was walking around the forest, she heard something growling in the bushes. She stopped walking and said, "Who's there?"

Suddenly, a big creature jumped out of the bushes and pinned her down! The creature roared at Victoria. Instead of crying, Victoria looked at the creature straight in the eye and roared back! Surprised, the creature jumped back and let Victoria go. The little elf stood up and brushed the dirt off her clothes. Then she looked at the creature that jumped at her and said, "It's not nice to pounce on other creatures like that."

The creature looked at Victoria and said, "I'm sorry?"

"Are you asking me or are you telling me that you're sorry?" Victoria asked in a challenging tone. Now that she got a good look at the creature, Victoria realized that she didn't know what the creature was. It had the body of a lion but the head and wings of an eagle. "What are you?" Victoria asked.

"I'm a griffin and my name is Diego," the griffin answered.

"I've never met a griffin before," Victoria said. Then she smiled at Diego and continued, "It's nice to meet you. My name is Victoria and I'm an elf."

"You're so small. Aren't you afraid of me?" Diego asked.

"No, I'm not. But should I be afraid of you? Are you going to eat me?" Victoria asked.

"Of course, not!" Diego said. "I was just practicing my pouncing so I jumped out of the bushes. But griffins don't eat elves."

"That's good to know," Victoria said. "Can you fly?"

"Of course," Diego said, "I have wings, after all. How about you?"

"No, I can't. Fairies have wings so they can fly but us elves, we get around by walking," Victoria explained. Then she asked, "Are you new to this forest?"

"Yes," Diego said, "we live in a different forest and we seldom come down to the ground. If you get around by walking, griffins like me get around by flying."

"That's so cool," Victoria said. "Do you want me to show you around?"

"Sure," answered Diego, "hop up on my back, I can carry you."

Victoria climbed on Diego's back, up to his neck, and she sat on his head. Then the two new friends explored the forest. While exploring, Victoria shared stories about the different parts of the forest to Diego. When they reached the edge of the forest, they continued walking until they reached a cliff.

"I guess this is where our exploration ends," Victoria said.

"It doesn't have to end," said Diego.

"What do you mean?" asked Victoria.

Diego spread his wings and asked, "Do you want to fly with me?"

"Really?" Victoria said. She had never tried flying before. The thought of flying made her feel excited. Then she answered, "Yes, please!"

As soon as Victoria answered, Diego took off and started flying. Victoria was amazed at how it felt! They soared through the sky and up into the clouds. Victoria didn't say anything while they were flying. She was too busy appreciating the beauty of the sky. When they landed, Victoria hopped off Diego's head and said, "Thank you, that was wonderful."

"No problem," Diego answered, "I can come back again tomorrow and we can continue exploring."

"That sounds great, Diego. See you tomorrow," Victoria said. From that day on, the two friends explored all the parts of the land and sky together and they always had a lot of fun while exploring.

Icky, Mucky, Mud

Leah the unicorn has traveled all over her forest home. Since she didn't have any brothers or sisters, she wasn't very friendly. Leah preferred to spend time by herself exploring the different parts of the forest. One day, while Leah was exploring, she reached a part of the forest that she had never seen before. It was covered in trees and it looked dark inside.

Slowly, Leah stepped into the darkness and saw that she came into a swamp. Leah looked around but she didn't see any other creatures around. The young unicorn walked around the swamp to see the surroundings. But even though Leah was careful, she slipped and fell right into the mud!

"Oh!" Leah cried out. The mud was so slippery and thick that Leah couldn't move. Leah struggled as she tried crawling out of the mud but it was no use.

Just when Leah thought that she was going to sink into the mud, she felt someone grab her.

"Pull, Ben!" said one voice.

"I am pulling!" said another.

After a while, Leah was out of the mud. She lay on the ground breathing hard.

"Are you okay?" asked one of the voices Leah heard while she was sinking in the mud.

The young unicorn opened her eyes and saw two slimy monsters staring at her. Leah opened her eyes in surprise and asked, "What are you?" Leah saw that her question hurt the feelings of the two monsters. She felt bad about that so she said, "I'm sorry, I was just surprised. Thank you for saving me. My name is Leah."

The two monsters smiled at Leah then one of them said, "I'm Ben and this is Felix."

"It's nice to meet you," Leah said. Then she asked, "Are you... swamp monsters?"

"Yes," Ben said. We were watching you when you came into our swamp. We have never seen a unicorn before."

"He's right," Felix agreed, "usually, unicorns don't like coming into the swamp because it's so slimy and full of mud."

"It's my first time to come into this swamp. I didn't know how slippery the ground was," Leah said.

"A lot of creatures slip into the mud. That's why we swamp monsters sit here. We guard the swamp to help creatures that fall in," Ben explained.

"Do you ever leave the swamp?" Leah asked.

Felix looked down and said, "No, we're not allowed to."

"We smell like the swamp so other creatures won't want to come near us anyway," Ben said sadly.

"Does that mean that you don't know what the world looks like outside of this swamp?" Leah asked again.

"That's right," said Ben.

Leah thought for a few moments about how these monsters saved her life. Then she had a great idea! "Why don't I tell you stories about the outside world?" Leah asked.

"Really?" Felix asked.

"Yes! It's the least I can do after you saved me. At least you would know all about the outside world even if you don't get to explore it on your own," Leah said.

The two swamp monsters sat in front of the young unicorn. She shared stories about the world, the trees, the flowers, the lakes, and everything else she could remember. Leah even told them about some of her adventures as she explored the different parts of the forest. Soon, the sun started to set and Leah had to go back home.

"Will you come back?" Felix asked.

"Yes, I will," Leah said. This made the two monsters happy. As she left the swamp, Ben and Felix went back to their hiding spot. Meanwhile, Leah went home thinking about how nice it was to meet new friends while exploring.

Our Beautiful World

On a beautiful summer day, a group of friends sat together sharing stories. This was a unique group as it consisted of different creatures. Sitting in the circle was Hannah the centaur, Mia the fairy, Jane the elf, Aaron the dwarf, and Paul the unicorn. The young creatures talked about the beauty of the world and how they all lived in harmony.

"I still can't believe how the different creatures used to be at war with each other," Hannah said. She remembered the stories their teacher told them about the history of their world. In the past, the different creatures fought with each other until one day, the elders came together to make peace.

"It's a good thing our elders found a way to make peace," said Aaron, "otherwise, we won't even be friends!"

Out of nowhere, Paul asked, "Have you guys seen the part of the forest which got burned?"

All the other creatures looked at Paul in surprise and Jane said, "Is there such a place?"

"Yes," said Paul, "in that place, the eldest unicorn died in the fire. Nobody knows how the fire started. But when the eldest unicorn died, that was when all the other elders decided to make peace."

"Can you take us there, Paul?" Mia asked.

"Sure," said Paul. Then the whole group of friends stood up and started following Paul. After about half an hour, they reached their destination. The young creatures stood together quietly. This part of the forest was dark, sad, and silent. It wasn't like all the other parts of the forest which were full of life and colors.

"This is so sad," Mia said.

"Can't we do something about it?" Jane asked her friends.

"What if we try to fix it?" Aaron asked.

"How will we do that?" Paul asked.

Everyone stopped talking. They were all thinking about what they can do to heal this part of the forest. After a few moments, Hannah said, "We can start by cleaning it up."

The rest of them agreed. They went into the forest and started picking up the scattered leaves, twigs, branches, and other burned items. Then they took water from a nearby lake and poured it on the ground. Right before lunchtime, the group of friends was done cleaning up. As they admired their work, someone said, "Wow, you guys did an amazing job!"

The friends saw that Paul's Mom had arrived. She smiled at them and pointed at a basket of fruits. She said, "I saw you cleaning up on my way home. I picked fruits from our garden for your lunch."

"Thank you!" said the young creatures as they shared the fruits. While having lunch, the young creatures talked about what they would do next. It was Mia's idea to plant trees the next day. They even planned to call their other friends to help out.

It only took one week for all the young creatures in the forest to transform the burned area into something bright and vibrant. Now, the whole forest had become a beautiful place to live in. Some creatures even decided to move into that part of the forest. The group of young creatures were able to make a difference in the world and they did this by helping each other out.

Learning Is Fun!

Chapter 7:
Learning Is Fun!

All our lives, we learn new things. For children, learning is one of the most important things in life. You want your child to learn the right values, basic skills, and even things that they need to excel in school. If your child develops a love for learning, this will make things much easier for them and for you. This chapter helps emphasize the fact that learning can be fun. Hopefully, your child will feel more excited about learning after hearing these stories.

Big and Small

Madison and Jade were the unlikeliest of friends. Madison was a dwarf while Jade was a giant but they were closer than sisters. When they were still young, Madison helped Jade out of a tough spot. Jade was exploring outside of Giant Village when her legs got tangled in vines. Since her fingers were too big, Jade couldn't untangle the vines. It's a good thing Madison came along. She carefully untangled the knotted vines to free the young giant. Since then, Madison and Jade have become best friends.

"Hi, Jade!" Madison called out while waving at her best friend.

Jade looked up and saw her little friend running towards her. Jade smiled and said, "Hi, Madison! I'm almost ready."

The little dwarf stopped in front of the giant and waited patiently. She couldn't wait to visit the Wise Willow Tree with her best friend. After Jade tied her shoes and zipped her bag, Jade stood up and said, "I'm ready. Let's go!"

Madison and Jade went on their way. Most creatures who saw them wondered how a dwarf and a giant could be such close friends. Sometimes, creatures would even tease them but this didn't bother the pair. They always supported each other no matter what.

Today, Madison and Jade were on their way to the Wise Willow Tree. This was an old tree in the forest that told stories to young creatures about the past. Through these stories, Madison and Jade learned a lot of things. One time, they learned that giants used to be scary, ruthless creatures until they destroyed the village of a very powerful fairy. The fairy cursed the giants and made them small. When the whole village apologized to the fairy, she forgave them but on one condition. That they promised to respect other creatures no matter how small.

For Madison, her favorite story was about the dwarf who went on an adventure to learn how big the world was. The dwarf walked on land, sailed on water, and even flew in the sky with the help of griffins and flying unicorns. When he went back home, the dwarf wrote a book about his adventures and the Wise Willow Tree had memorized them all. At least once a week, Madison and Jade visited the old tree to hear her stories and learn new things.

When they arrived, Madison and Jade joined the group of young creatures who were sitting around the Wise Willow Tree. "Good morning, Wise Willow Tree," said Madison and Jade together. The old tree looked at them and smiled. Then she said, "Ah, my favorite pair of friends. Please sit down. Today, I will tell you a story about two friends just like Madison and Jade."

The Wise Willow Tree told the young creatures a story about a fire fairy who became friends with a mermaid. Even though they had opposite elements, they found ways to spend time together and grow closer to each other. Their families didn't want the fire fairy and the mermaid to be best friends because they had always hated each other. But when their families saw how much these two creatures loved each other, they learned to accept the unique friendship they had. Now that Madison and Jade heard this story, they had a new favorite as it was all about an unlikely friendship just like theirs.

My First Day of Wizard School

When George woke up, he felt butterflies in his stomach. George is a young wizard and today was his first day of Wizard School. George bounded out of bed and brushed his teeth. Then he grabbed his backpack and his wand and ran down to the dining room.

"Good morning, mom. Good morning, Dad," George said excitedly.

His parents smiled then his Mom said, "Aren't you happy this morning!"

"Of course, mom. Today is my first day of school," George replied.

"Did you bring everything on your list?" his Dad asked.

"Yes, I prepared my things last night before going to bed," George said.

As they were having breakfast, George's parents talked about their experiences in school. Just like all other witches and wizards, his parents learned almost everything they knew in school. Now, they were both very successful and both of them were excited to see George go to school too.

When they were done, George left the house with his dad. George's Dad would drop him off at school before going to work. "Bye, mom," George said.

"Goodbye, George," answered his mom, "have fun at school."

While walking to school, the butterflies in his stomach seemed to flutter around more. He realized that he was feeling nervous. George looked up at his Dad and said, "Dad, were you nervous during your first day of school?"

"Why do you ask, son?" said his dad.

"Oh, nothing," George replied.

George's Dad smiled and asked, "Are you feeling nervous, George?"

The young wizard looked down and said, "I-I think so."

George's Dad chuckled softly. Then he said, "It's okay to feel nervous, George. But when I was young, I didn't feel nervous during my first day of school. I felt terrified!"

George looked up at his Dad once again and said, "Really?"

"Yes," said his dad, "and you can even ask grandpa about it when you see him. I never liked the idea of going to school. I begged my Dad to teach me magic so that I didn't have to go to school. Of course, your grandpa didn't want me to miss school."

"Wow," George said with wonder. "I can't imagine you feeling scared, Dad."

"Well, I was," George's Dad said. "I even cried when my Dad dropped me off at school. I kicked and screamed all the way to my classroom. Even when I was inside the classroom, I wouldn't stop crying."

"You spent your whole first day crying?" George asked.

"No," his Dad answered with a laugh. "Back then, I had a wonderful teacher. She sat next to me and told me a story about being brave. While listening to my teacher's story, I didn't realize that I had already stopped crying. When she was done, the bell rang and my teacher led me to my seat. When I sat down, your uncle Jimmy introduced himself and we became friends right away."

"That's nice," George said.

"My point is that school can be scary but it's also a lot of fun. As long as you learn how to be brave, you can see past your fears and realize what school is really about," George's Dad said.

"Thanks, Dad," George said. They had reached the school and the butterflies in George's stomach were gone. He was now excited as he walked up the steps to enjoy his first day.

Learning How to Fly

Luna the griffin sat down in a circle with the other young griffins in school. Usually, Luna loved school but today, she was feeling a bit sleepy. She knew that she was going to learn how to fly today and the thought kept her up all night. Luna tried to practice flying on her own but she never got the hang of it. Because of this, she felt like her wings were too weak. So when her teacher told her the day before that they were going to learn how to fly today, Luna was scared.

"Luna, are you listening?" her teacher asked.

Luna looked at her teacher with wide eyes and said, "Y-yes. I'm listening."

"You don't seem like yourself today. Are you okay?" her teacher asked again.

"I just feel a bit sleepy," Luna admitted. "I was up almost half the night thinking about our flying lesson."

Luna's teacher smiled warmly and said, "Were you scared?"

"Yes," Luna said, feeling shy. Her teacher looked at everyone else and asked, "Is anyone else feeling scared about learning how to fly today?"

One by one, all of her classmates raised their paws. She looked around and realized that they were all feeling nervous about learning this skill. Luna's teacher chuckled softly and said, "Alright, put your paws down, and let's talk about flying."

"Today, you have all reached the age when griffins learn how to fly," Luna's teacher began. "Just like you, I felt nervous when that day came. But there is a very important secret you should all know about flying."

"What is the secret?" Luna asked.

"Instinct," her teacher said. "The reason we wait until you reach a certain age is that griffins only get our natural instinct to fly at the age you are now. Once you get this instinct, you will learn how to fly without even trying!"

Luna suddenly felt awake and alert. No wonder she couldn't fly no matter how much she practiced. Even if she stretched her wings and flapped them as hard as she could, Luna always fell to the ground. Now that she knew the secret of flying, Luna didn't feel scared anymore. Now, she felt excited!

"I see that you're all excited now," Luna's teacher said happily. "We might as well start our flying lesson then!"

Luna's teacher stood up and told them to form a line. Then they walked together towards Flight Peak where all griffins learned how to fly. One by one, Luna's teacher asked the young griffins to step off the cliff and soar into the sky. Luna watched as her classmates learned how to fly using their instinct.

When it was her turn, Luna stopped at the edge of the cliff and down at the ground below. She closed her eyes, took a deep breath, and stepped off the cliff. As she was falling, she spread her wings and flapped them. She opened her eyes and smiled as she realized that she was flying. It was the best feeling ever and Luna was happy to finally learn this skill that all griffins possessed naturally.

Patience Is a Virtue

Simon was a very playful troll. He played by himself, he played with his friends, and he also played with his brothers and sisters. All day, Simon would play until it was time to go to bed. Only then would Simon be still.

"Good morning, family!" Simon said happily as he entered the dining room. He was always the last one to wake up because he was the most tired of them all. When he sat down to have breakfast, he saw that all of his brothers and sisters were almost done eating.

"We're going to play by the lake today, Simon," said one of his brothers. Then they all took one last bite of their breakfast and stood up. They placed their plates and glasses in the sink and ran out the door. "You can follow us at the lake when you're done, Simon," said his eldest sister before she left.

"That's not fair!" Simon cried out.

His Mom smiled at him and patted his head affectionately, "That's what you get for waking up late, Simon."

Feeling a bit upset, Simon finished his breakfast. Then he tidied up his plate and ran out the door. On his way to the lake, Simon decided to play by himself today. He ran into the forest to climb trees. This was one of his favorite past times. He would climb the trees and jump from one treetop to another by swinging on vines. Today, Simon wasn't paying attention because he was still feeling upset. Because he was distracted, Simon missed one of the vines and fell to the ground!

"Ouch!" Simon cried out. He could feel pain in his leg. Simon tried to stand up but the pain was too strong. "Help!" he cried out. A few moments later, Simon heard footsteps running towards him. He turned his head and saw his brothers and sisters.

"What happened?" asked one of his brothers.

"I fell," Simon said.

"We're sorry we left you behind but let us help you now," said his eldest sister. Together, they carried Simon home. Once there, Simon's Dad wrapped his leg in leaves and twigs. Then he said, "You shouldn't get up for at least three days for your leg to heal, Simon."

"Three days?" Simon said. "That's like forever!"

Simon's Dad smiled at him and said, "You have to learn how to be patient, son. Otherwise, you might break your leg and when that happens, it will take a longer time for you to heal."

Patience wasn't something Simon had. But for three days, he had no choice. He sat by the window and watched as young creatures in his neighborhood played in the streets. Simon tried to distract himself by doing other things but he still wanted to play outside. As the hours went by, Simon started to realize the importance of patience. He understood that if he tried to force himself to play, he might get hurt more. So Simon decided to wait patiently. After three days, his patience paid off as his leg healed and he was able to play outside again!

Important Values To Learn

Chapter 8:
Important Values To Learn

As children grow up, there are certain values they must learn. Beyond reading, writing, mathematics, and other academic subjects, these values will ensure that your child grows up to be a kind, responsible adult. In this chapter, your child will learn some of the most important values learned through the eyes of memorable characters.

Clean Up Your Mess

Ashley the mermaid was one of the most untidy mermaids in Mermaid Cove. Although she was very smart and popular, she always made a mess wherever she went. Whether at home or in school, Ashley never cleaned anything up.

One day, Ashley planned to spend the whole morning making a project for school. Over the weekend, Ashley's teacher told the class to create a model of a coral reef using different kinds of underwater plants. Ashley spent an hour gathering all of the materials she needed for her project. She scattered them all over the front of their house, sat down, and started working. After some time, Ashley's Mom came out of the house and said, "Ashley, take a break for a while. It's time for lunch."

Ashley looked up and smiled at her mom. She was almost done with her project. After lunch, she just had to add the finishing touches. Then, she can go and play with her friends. "Alright, mom," Ashley said.

Before going back inside the house, Ashley's Mom reminded her, "Don't forget to clean up first." But the young mermaid wasn't listening. She was tying a piece of string around a strip of kelp to attach it to one of the plant corals she had made. When she was done, she left her project outside and swam into their house to have lunch with her family.

When she was done, Ashley swam back outside to finish her project. But she was shocked to see little fish nibbling on her coral reef! "Oh, no!" Ashley cried out. She swam towards her project and scared the tiny fish away. When Ashley saw her project, she started crying. The small fish had eaten most of the plants she used and now, all that was left was the frame of her coral reef.

Ashley's Mom swam next to her and said, "I heard you cry out. What happened?"

"The fish ate my project, mom!" Ashley cried as she gave her Mom a hug. "I worked so hard on that project and now I have to start over!"

"But, didn't I tell you to clean up before coming in for lunch?" Ashley's Mom asked her.

"I didn't hear you say that. Maybe I wasn't listening," Ashley said. She wiped her tears away. Ashley's Mom said, "This is why it's important to clean your messes, Ashley. You should learn how to be more responsible so that things like this don't happen."

"Alright, mom," Ashley said.

"Now, shall we work on your project together?" Ashley's Mom asked.

"Really? You'll help me?" Ashley asked her mom.

"Of course!" she said. "As long as you promise me that you will clean up from now on and try to be more responsible."

"I promise, mom," Ashley said. Then they started working on her project together.

I Didn't Do It!

Caleb the yeti felt scared. He was playing around the house when he bumped into one of the shelves and broke his dad's favorite trophy. He was alone at home because his parents went out to look for food. Caleb picked up the broken trophy and almost cried. His Dad will be furious when he comes home!

"What am I going to do," Caleb said to himself. His parents always warned him not to run around inside the house because he might break something or even hurt himself. But whenever he was left alone at home, Caleb couldn't resist. He always jumped and ran around the house while imagining that he was an explorer.

Caleb the yeti tried to think about how he could get out of this mess. Then he had a bright idea! He put the broken trophy back on the floor and opened the door. After that, Caleb went to his room and waited for his parents to come back. Hours later, Caleb heard his Dad call out to him, "Caleb, we're home!"

Still feeling scared, Caleb went outside to meet his parents. He saw his Dad standing over the broken trophy. He said, "Oh no, what happened here?"

"I didn't do it!" Caleb said right away.

His Dad looked at him and said, "But you were the only one here."

"Maybe you left the door open and the wind blew your trophy off the shelf," Caleb reasoned.

"He might be right," his Mom said gently. "When we came home, the door was wide open."

Caleb looked at his dad. He felt bad as his Dad picked up the pieces of the broken trophy. He had a sad expression on his face. Caleb knew that his Dad loved that trophy and now, it was gone.

"Alright, get cleaned up. Your Mom and I brought home your favorite dinner," Caleb's Dad said as he picked up the last pieces of the broken trophy.

"Okay, Dad," Caleb said. After washing his hands, Caleb joined his parents at the table. His Dad still looked sad even when they started eating. Caleb couldn't take it anymore. He said, "Dad, I'm sorry."

Caleb's Dad looked at him and said, "What for, Caleb?"

"I-I broke your trophy," the young yeti admitted. "I didn't mean it, Dad. It was an accident."

Both of his parents were looking at him now. Then his Mom said, "You should have told us the truth from the start."

"I know," Caleb said, "I'm really sorry. I promise never to lie again."

Caleb's Dad smiled. "I might have lost my favorite trophy but I am happy that you learned the importance of honesty."

It's Okay If You're Not Okay

Emily the witch loved going to school. She had a best friend, her teachers were nice, and she loved learning new spells. Every day, she felt excited to go to school, especially since her best friend Krista lived right next door. On her way to school, she would pass by Krista's house and wait for her outside. Then the two young witches walked to school together while talking about different things.

One sunny day, Emily left the house after saying goodbye to her parents. She wanted to tell Krista all about the funny thing that happened last night while she was having dinner with her family. She walked down the street and stopped right in front of her best friend's house. She waited and waited. Then she waited some more. But for some reason, Krista didn't come out!

Emily walked up to Krista's house and knocked on the front door. When the door opened, Emily saw Krista's mom. She said, "Hello! I have been waiting outside for Krista so that we can go to school."

"Oh," Krista's Mom said, "I'm so sorry, Emily but Krista will not be coming to school today."

"Why?" Emily asked.

"She's not feeling well. I'm sorry you had to wait," Krista's Mom said.

"That's okay. Please tell Krista that I stopped by and I hope she feels better soon," said Emily. Krista's Mom smiled, nodded, and closed the door.

When Emily walked to school, she felt sad. This was the first time that she would be going to school on her own. Her sadness followed her all the way to class. Emily's teacher noticed how sad Emily was so she asked, "Emily, what's wrong?"

"Oh, it's nothing," Emily said as she gave her teacher a smile. She didn't want anyone to see that she wasn't okay. After a while, one of her classmates asked her again, "Emily, what's wrong?"

Again, Emily smiled and said, "I'm okay."

Emily looked at Krista's empty chair and felt even sadder. Just then, Sophia, the quietest girl in class, came up to Emily. She said, "You miss Krista, don't you?"

"Oh," Emily said, "yes, but it's okay. I'm okay."

"You know," Sophia said, "it's okay if you're not okay. You don't have to pretend that you're okay all the time even if you feel sad." Then the young witch smiled at Emily and went back to her seat.

Emily was surprised at how kind Sophia was. Since she was always with Krista, she never spent time with her other classmates. Emily stood up, walked towards Sophia, and sat down in the chair next to her. Then she said, "Thank you, Sophia. You made me feel better." That day, Emily made a new friend all because another witch showed her genuine kindness.

We Can Do This Together

Two unicorns named Marie and Dylan were exploring the forest one day when they saw something shiny up in a tree. "What is it?" Marie said.

"I don't know," answered Dylan, "it's too far high up in the tree for me to see it clearly."

"Maybe it's something magical!" Marie exclaimed with excitement.

"Well, even if it is, we can't get it," Dylan said with disappointment.

"What if we ask for help?" Maria asked her brother.

Dylan looked around but he didn't see any other creatures in the forest. He said, "But we're the only ones here."

Marie sighed. She looked up at the shiny object. Just then, the two unicorns heard voices behind the trees. They walked towards the sound of the voices to see who was there. Behind the trees, Marie and Dylan saw three forest fairies playing with each other.

"Hello," Marie said.

The three fairies stopped playing and looked at the unicorns. One of the boy fairies said, "Hi. Who are you?"

"My name is Marie and this is my brother, Dylan," said the unicorn with a smile.

"Hello, Marie and Dylan," answered the girl fairy. "My name is Abby and these are my brothers, Aaron and Jay."

"It's nice to meet you," Dylan said.

Then Marie said, "Can we ask for your help?"

"With what?" asked Jay.

"Come on, follow us," Marie said as she and Dylan galloped back to the tree where the shiny object was. Then she pointed up and said, "My brother and I saw something shiny up there but we can't see what it is. Can you please fly up there to see it?"

"Sure," said Abby who flew up to the top of the tree. After a few moments, she came back down and said, "It's a crown! But how did it get all the way up there?"

"Hey," Aaron said, "do you think it's the crown of the water fairy queen? I heard an eagle snatched her crown a few days ago."

"That might be it!" Marie said excitedly.

"If it is, we should try to get it so that we can give it back to her," Dylan said.

"We can definitely do it if we work together," Jay said with a smile.

So the unicorns and fairies came up with a plan. Since the crown was too big for the three young fairies to carry, they would fly up to shake it off the branches. When it falls down, the two unicorns will catch the crown using a large leaf that they will hold together.

After making their plan, the young creatures worked together to get the crown. Their plan worked so well and soon, they had the crown in the leaf. "Let's go give it back," Marie said. The other creatures agreed. They walked together towards the lake to return the crown to the queen of the water fairies. When they reached the lake, the water fairy immediately saw her crown and said, "You found my crown!"

The two unicorns and three fairies bowed in front of the queen of the water fairies. Then she said, "Please rise. Come and join us as we celebrate the return of my crown. Thank you for bringing it back to me."

"You're welcome," Marie said.

"We're happy to help," Dylan said. "And we're also happy that we made new friends along the way."

I Am Special

Chapter 9:

I Am Special

All children are special. As a parent, nurturing and encouraging your child will make them feel special and unique. Instead of trying to get children to conform, it's better to celebrate their differences. This helps children grow up to be kind and accepting. In this chapter, your child will learn that being unique is a good thing and they all have something special to share.

I Am Different and That's Okay

Gabe the fairy went to school with all the other fairies. He was one of the most popular fairies in his class because he was confident, friendly, and he enjoyed spending time with his friends. Sometimes, when some of the fairies in the class had trouble understanding the lessons, Gabe was always willing to help them out.

"Hi, guys!" Gabe said to his classmates as he went into the classroom. All of his classmates waved at him and some of them replied to his greeting. Gabe went straight to his seat in the class. He turned to his seatmate, a fairy named

Coral, and they started talking. But when the bell rang, all of the young fairies grew silent when their teacher came inside.

"Good morning, class," said their teacher.

"Good morning, Ms. Blossom," the class answered.

"I have some exciting news today," Ms. Blossom said excitedly. "In a few minutes, we will be welcoming a new fairy in our class. She is a night fairy and this is her first time to study with daytime fairies. So please try to welcome her as warmly as possible."

Right after Ms. Blossom talked about their new classmate, a soft knock came on the door. Ms. Blossom opened the door and Gabe saw their new classmate standing outside. She had pale, white skin, jet-black hair, and bright yellow eyes. The whole class was quiet as the new fairy came inside. Ms. Blossom led her to the front of the class and said, "Welcome! Please introduce yourself."

The young night fairy stood in front of the class without smiling. Then she said, "My name is Amaya and I am a fairy of the night." The whole class waited for her to say more but she just stood there quietly. "Okay then," Ms. Blossom said after a while. "You may find a seat where you will feel comfortable," she continued. There were many seats available but Amaya chose to sit at the back.

Ms. Blossom started teaching the class and Gabe listened with the rest of his classmates until the recess bell rang. Then all of the young fairies stood up and walked out of the classroom. Gabe was the first to step outside but he stood next to the door and waited for Amaya to come out. When the last fairy came out, he didn't see Amaya. Gabe peeked inside the classroom and saw that the young night fairy was still sitting at the back while staring at the window.

Gabe went inside the classroom and approached Amaya. He sat down next to Amaya and said, "Hi, my name is Gabe."

Amaya looked at Gabe and gave him a small smile but she didn't say anything. So Gabe continued, "Do you want to hang out with me and the other fairies outside?"

"No, thank you," Amaya said.

"That's okay," Gabe answered, "but can I sit here with you?"

"Why? Do the other fairies make fun of you too?" Amaya asked.

"What do you mean?" Gabe asked, feeling surprised.

"You're different from them just like me. In my old school, they always teased me for being different," Amaya said.

In fact, Gabe was different from the other fairies. While most of the fairies in their class were from the forest, Gabe saw from the desert. But ever since he went to school, nobody ever teased him about it.

"Yes, I am different and so are you," Gabe said, "but in this school, it's okay to be different. Nobody has ever teased me about standing out. In fact, a lot of the fairies were super interested to learn more about me when I first came here."

Amaya looked at Gabe and asked, "Really?"

"Yes," Gabe answered, "that's why I love this school. Everyone here is so kind and accepting. Come on, let me introduce you to our classmates."

Amaya smiled shyly and said, "Okay." She was happy to find a school where she could be herself no matter how different she was.

It's Okay To Feel Bad Sometimes

Samantha the dwarf was the happiest dwarf in the land. Whenever she came into a room, all other dwarves and creatures immediately felt happy just because she was there. Samantha knew how to make others laugh and she always knew what to say to make others feel better.

Wherever Samantha went, she would be accompanied by her pet hedgehog. Two years ago, Samantha found the little hedgehog in their garden. The poor hedgehog was trapped in a bush and she helped him out. Since then, the little hedgehog never left Samantha's side. When she realized that he had become her pet, Samantha named the hedgehog, Ash.

One day, Samantha woke up and said, "Good morning!" to her pet. Then she got up, fixed her bed, and went straight to the dining room to have breakfast. "Good morning, Mom and dad," Samantha said. Then she sat down and started eating.

"Good morning, Samantha," her Dad said.

"Good morning, dear. Where is Ash?" her Mom asked.

Samantha stopped eating and looked at the plate right next to hers. Usually, her little pet would already be eating right next to her. "That's strange," she said. Then Samantha stood up and excused herself. She went back to her room and called out to her pet. But Ash wasn't in his little bed.

Samantha started to feel worried. She looked for the tiny hedgehog and said, "Ash?" When she lifted her pillow, she saw Ash huddled in the corner of her bed. She gently took the little hedgehog from the bed and brought him closer to her face, "Hey, Ash, are you okay?"

The hedgehog shivered. Samantha ran back to the dining room and said, "Mom! Dad! Something's wrong with Ash!"

She gently placed her pet on the table for her parents to see. Her Mom said, "Did you find him like this?"

"Y-yes," Samantha said. She wanted to cry but she was trying to be strong for Ash. Samantha's Mom pet the little hedgehog gently and tried to wake him up. But again, Ash just shivered.

"I think we need to bring him to the vet," Samantha's Dad said. The whole family tidied up their breakfast dishes and brought Ash to the vet. Once there, the vet took the little hedgehog inside the clinic and he asked Samantha and her parents to wait in the waiting area. While waiting, Samantha tried to hide her worry by talking about school, her friends, and anything under the sun.

But when the vet took too long to come out, Samantha couldn't control herself anymore. She said, "May I please go outside? I think I need some air."

"Okay, Samantha," her Mom said.

The young dwarf ran outside, took a deep breath, and started crying. She was very worried about Ash. Since she found the hedgehog in their garden, they had been inseparable. She couldn't imagine what she would do if something bad happened to Ash.

A few moments later, Samantha's Mom came out and said, "Are you okay, Samantha?"

She quickly wiped her tears and said, "I'm okay, mom."

Samantha's Mom gave her a hug and said, "You know, it's okay for you to not feel okay sometimes, especially when things like this happen."

"But other creatures always say that they love me because I'm always happy. I want to be strong for Ash so I want to be happy," Samantha said.

"It's okay to feel sad or worried sometimes but that doesn't mean that you're not strong," her Mom said. Now that Samantha knew that she didn't have to put on a happy face all the time, she gave her Mom a tight hug and cried. Her Mom hugged her tighter and smiled at how strong her young daughter was.

Finding Confidence

"Good morning, Gabby!" said Gabby's Mom as she entered the young dragon's den.

"Hello, mom," Gabby said. She was already sitting down and looking outside as the sun started to rise.

"Oh, you're awake!" Gabby's Mom said happily. "Are you excited to go to school?"

"Not really, mom," Gabby said. "Can I just rest today and go to school tomorrow?"

Gabby's Mom was worried about the young dragon. Their family had just moved from a land far away. In Gabby's old school, she was the smallest dragon. Because of this, the other young dragons used to tease her about her size. This made Gabby very shy and self-conscious. She didn't have any friends and she didn't enjoy school at all.

Then Gabby's parents heard about the school in this land. Here, different kinds of dragons attended the school. There were dragons from different lands and dragons of different species and they all got along well. The teachers in the school encouraged the young dragons to accept each other no matter how different they are from one another. Before moving to this new land, Gabby's parents visited the school and what they saw made them happy. Young dragons of different shapes and sizes were playing, chatting, and flying together. They knew that Gabby would fit into the school perfectly.

"Why don't you give this school a chance, Gabby? You might be surprised," her Mom said.

"But I'm not feeling well, mom," Gabby said.

"What are you feeling?" her Mom asked.

"I-I don't know," Gabby admitted. "I just don't want to go to school."

Gabby's Mom gave her a hug. She didn't want to force her daughter to go to school but at the same time, she wanted her daughter to give the school a try. Just then, Gabby's Dad came into the den. "Hello, Gabby. Ready for school?" he asked. Gabby's Mom looked at him and shook her head.

"Oh," Gabby's Dad said then he sat down next to Gabby too. "You know, Gabby, your Mom and I visited the school before we moved here. And do you know what we saw?"

"What?" Gabby asked.

"We saw all types of dragons there! Dark-colored dragons, light-colored dragons, scaly dragons, furry dragons, enormous dragons, and even small ones," he said.

"Wow," Gabby said as her eyes grew wide. "Is that true?" she asked her mom.

"Yes," Gabby's Mom confirmed, "that's why we chose the school here. Because we know that you will fit in wonderfully."

"So let me ask you again, are you ready for school?" Gabby's Dad asked.

"I guess so," Gabby said shyly.

The three dragons flew all the way to Gabby's new school. On the way, she saw other young dragons flying with their parents. When they reached the school, Gabby saw that her parents were right. There were different types of dragons here. Some of them were even smaller than her! The more Gabby observed the dragons at the school, the more confident she felt.

"Let's go meet your teacher, Gabby," her Mom said.

When Gabby saw her teacher, she smiled. Her teacher had the same colored scales as her. She was also very beautiful. The teacher said, "Hello, Gabby. It's lovely to meet you."

"H-hello," Gabby replied. Then her parents greeted her teacher too. "I know you will be happy here, Gabby. Do you have any special talents you want to share?"

"Oh," Gabby said.

"It's okay, Gabby," her Mom said, "you can show her."

Gabby was a very special dragon but she never had the chance to show others how special she was just because she was too small. But now, as she looked around, she knew that this school was special just like her. Gabby smiled and breathed blue-colored flames. Very few dragons could do this and now, Gabby found the confidence to share this special talent with others.

Learning How To Speak Up

Elves are known for being calm, peaceful, and harmonious. Just like all other young elves, Max already possessed all of these qualities. While elves are very young, they practice different kinds of meditation techniques to help them learn how to become peaceful, harmonious, and calm.

Max was a very smart elf which is why his teacher invited him to join the exchange student program at the goblin school. "Goblins?" Max asked.

"Yes," his teacher said, "the goblin school is the most challenging school to go to but I believe you can handle it."

"Okay," Max said even though he wasn't sure about spending a week in a school filled with goblins. While elves were known for peace and serenity, goblins were known for being mischievous tricksters. Still, Max agreed because he didn't want the leaders of the schools to end up fighting with each other.

On his first day at goblin school, Max went into a classroom filled with noisy, rowdy goblins. He felt shocked because this classroom was the exact opposite of the classroom at his school. Here, everything was messy, there were scribbles everywhere, and there was even a strange smell in the air. Max entered the room quietly and found an empty seat. When he sat down, the whole room became quiet. When he looked up, Max saw that all of the goblins were staring at him.

"What do we have here?" said one of the goblins.

"Who are you?" said another.

"My name is Max and I am here for the exchange student program," Max said.

"Wow! An exchange student!" said the first goblin. "Why did they choose you?"

"You have to ask my teachers about that," he said.

Suddenly, the goblins formed a circle around Max. But before they could say or do anything else, the teacher came in and said, "All right everyone, back to your seats."

When all the goblins sat down, Max was surprised to see that the teacher was an elf! She had long white hair, bright blue eyes, and a clear complexion. Compared to the young goblins, the teacher looked magical. She looked at Max and said, "I see that you have already arrived."

Max stood up and said, "Yes, good morning."

The elf teacher smiled and said, "Good morning, Max. I hope you learn a lot in the week that you will spend here."

Then the teacher started teaching and when Max looked around, he saw that all of the goblins were listening to her very carefully. Even though the classroom looked like a jungle when Max came in, it was now very quiet and orderly. When the recess bell rang and all of the goblins ran outside, Max walked up to the teacher.

"That was amazing," he said.

"What was amazing?" the teacher asked him.

"When I came into the class, all of the goblins were talking, jumping around, and teasing each other. But as soon as you came in, they all became quiet," Max said with wonder.

The teacher smiled at Max and said, "Do you want to know my secret?"

"Of course!" Max said with excitement. "This is something I can share with my other teachers when I go back."

"Well," said the teacher, "I learned how to speak up. Elves like us are taught to be quiet, calm, and peaceful. That was the kind of teacher I was when I first came here. None of the students listened to me and I almost gave up. But one day, I decided to speak up and since then, they started to listen."

"You just spoke up?" Max asked.

"Yes. If you know that you are right, you must learn how to speak up. Otherwise, other creatures will just push you around," the teacher explained. "Now, go and join the goblins outside. They're not as bad as you think once you get to know them."

Max learned something new that day and by following the teacher's advice, he was able to make friends with all the goblins in the class.

The Things That Truly Matter

Chapter 10:
The Things That Truly Matter

Life is beautiful and this is something you want your children to realize while they are growing up. Beyond material things, the greatest treasures we have in life are right in front of us. In this last chapter, your child will learn about the things that truly matter. These stories are meant to help your children appreciate what they have so that they can live a happier, more fulfilling life.

My Family Supports Me

Amanda and Luke became friends because they were both new students at the School of Witches and Wizards. Amanda was a young witch from a well-known family while Luke was a young wizard from one of the poorest families in the land. Despite their differences, the pair of magical children got along very well. They spent all day together at school and during the weekends, they would sometimes meet too.

One day, Amanda and Luke met by the edge of the darkest forest in the land. According to legends, an old witch lived there and the creatures who find the witch get to wish for anything they want. Even though Amanda and Luke didn't believe the stories before, they both wanted to make wishes. Amanda wanted her parents to have more time for her while Luke wanted his family to become richer.

"Are you ready, Luke?" Amanda asked her friend.

"Yes," Luke answered, "and remember, we should always stick together."

Amanda nodded then the two entered the dark forest. The deeper they went inside the forest, the darker it became. Then Amanda took out her wand and said a magic spell for the tip of her wand to light up. Luke smiled at Amanda and gave her a thumbs up. Then they continued walking. Soon, they reached a clearing and in the middle of the clearing was a small, crooked house.

"Do you think that's it?" Luke said.

"Maybe," Amanda whispered. She was about to take another step when Luke stopped her. He said, "Wait, let me go inside first. I will see if it's safe. If I wave to you, that means you can follow me."

"Okay," Amanda said. She felt grateful to Luke because the truth was, she was feeling a bit scared. Luke bravely walked up to the house and knocked on the door. After a few moments, the door opened and a very old witch came out. Amanda watched as Luke talked to the witch. But then, the witch took out her wand and turned Luke to stone!

"Oh no, Luke!" Amanda cried out quietly. The witch used her wand to move Luke's statue to the side of her house where there were other statues there too. Amanda quickly stood up and ran all the way home. She opened the door to her house and called out to her parents, "Mom! Dad! I need help!"

After explaining what happened to Luke, Amanda and her parents went to Luke's house. Amanda told Luke's parents what happened then they all rushed to find the witch's house. Once there, Amana and Luke's parents knocked on the door and when the witch opened it, they all pointed their wands at her.

"Release Luke from the curse!" said Luke's dad.

The old witch said, "I am tired of young witches and wizards coming to my home asking for wishes!"

"We're sorry," Amanda said, "and we promise to spread the word about your wish to be left alone."

The witch looked at Amanda and said, "You promise?"

"Yes," Amanda said. The witch pointed her wand to the statues and in an instant, they were gone. She said, "They are now in their homes. Now, leave me be!" and she closed the door.

Amanda rushed to Luke's house along with Luke's parents and her own. When they got there, they saw Luke standing in front of the house. "Amanda! You're safe!" he said.

Amanda hugged him then looked at their parents. She said, "Thank you for helping us."

"Of course," Amanda's Mom said, "we are your family and we will always support you no matter what."

Beauty in Diversity

The story of Noah the centaur was known by all of the creatures in the land. One morning, the creatures woke up and saw a young centaur laying in the middle of a field. Nobody knew where he came from and when they asked him, Noah couldn't remember anything. Three months have passed since

Noah arrived but the young centaur was still too scared to talk to the other creatures.

"We should do something nice for Noah," Belle said. Belle was a griffin who was friends with all other creatures. Her best friend Helen was a dwarf and she said, "You're right. It has been three months and Noah just sits in the field. I think he's scared. Maybe he came from a land where there are only centaurs so he isn't used to talking to other creatures."

Francis the elf thought about what the two girls said. He used to be very shy too since he came from an Elf Forest where no other creatures lived. But when his family moved to this land, Francis learned to appreciate the beauty and wonder of living with different creatures. After some thought, Francis said, "Why don't we throw him a surprise party? Wouldn't that be fun?"

"That's a great idea!" Belle said.

"We can invite all the other young creatures and introduce them to Noah," Helen agreed.

Francis said, "We can have the party in the forest clearing next to the field. When everything is ready, I will invite Noah to explore with me, and lead him to the clearing."

The three friends planned the details of the party with excitement. When they were done, they ran to their friends' houses to share the details of their plan. All of the young creatures worked together to decorate the clearing and gather food for the party. Before the sun went down, they were done. They all went home after agreeing to meet in the clearing after the sun rises on the next day.

When morning came, the young creatures gathered in the clearing. Then Francis went to visit Noah in the field. "Hello, Noah," he said.

Noah looked at Francis and smiled. He already knew Francis because the young elf visited him sometimes. Francis would just sit with Noah and share stories. This made Noah feel good. "Hello, Francis," he said.

"I was wondering if you wanted to explore with me. It's such a beautiful day today," Francis said. Noah thought for a moment then said, "Okay, but let's not go too far." Francis nodded then he led Noah into the forest clearing. When they got there, the young creatures yelled, "Surprise!"

Indeed, Noah was surprised to see all of the young creatures there. He was so surprised that he almost galloped away. Then Belle walked up to Noah and said, "Welcome to our land, Noah. It has been months since you arrived and we wanted to welcome you officially. As you can see, we are all different from one another. But the differences we have made this land the most beautiful of all." Noah looked at the different creatures standing in front of him. Then he smiled as he saw that this diversity was, in fact, beautiful to see.

Seeing the Bright Side of Things

Chloe and Mia were monster sisters. Even though Chloe was older than Mia, they looked exactly alike. They both had yellow fur, orange spots, and big black eyes. These sisters were very close and they spent most of their time playing in a treehouse that their Dad built for them when they were young. In the treehouse, they pretended to be princesses, pirates, dragons, unicorns, and anything else they could imagine.

One day, Chloe and Mia were playing in their treehouse when they heard their Mom calling their names. They peeked down from the treehouse and saw their Mom standing on the ground. "Come inside, girls. It looks like a storm is coming," she said. The two monsters looked up at the sky and saw dark clouds.

"Uh-oh," Chloe said, "we'd better go inside the house, Mia. If it starts raining, we'll be drenched!"

Mia hated getting wet so she said, "Okay! Let's go!"

The two monster sisters quickly climbed down the tree and ran into their house. As soon as they closed the door, the rain started to pour outside. Then came strong flashes of lightning and loud bangs of thunder. Chloe saw that Mia was scared. She gave her little sister a hug and realized that she was shaking. "Don't be afraid, Mia. It's just lighting and thunder. We're safe here inside. Do you want to watch the storm from the window?"

Mia nodded her head and the two young monsters sat in front of their window. Chloe's arm was around her sister's shoulder as they watched the rain fall. Then a flash of lightning came and it set their treehouse on fire!

"Oh no!" Mia screamed.

"The treehouse!" Chloe screamed too.

Their parents ran to the window to see what the two monsters were screaming about. "Oh dear," said their Mom as they watched the whole treehouse burn down. Seeing their treehouse go up in flames made the two girls cry. They loved that treehouse and now, it was gone. Chloe and Mia's Mom hugged them while their Dad went into the kitchen.

When he came back, he was carrying two cups of hot chocolate, the favorite drink of the monster sisters. He gave them the mugs, closed the curtain, and sat down in front of the girls. They had just stopped crying but they still looked very sad. Then their Dad said, "I'm sorry about the treehouse girls. But you know what, there is a bright side to this."

"A bright side?" Chloe asked her dad.

"Yes. Sometimes, when bad things happen that we can't change, the best thing we can do is look on the bright side," their Dad said.

"But the treehouse burned down, Dad. What bright side do you see?" Mia asked.

He smiled at the girls warmly and said, "That treehouse was old. Now that it's gone, you can help me build a new one!"

Right away, the two girls smiled, "Really?" they said.

"Yes! This time, we will build a stronger treehouse where you can make more memories together. How does that sound?" their Dad asked.

The two girls jumped for joy! Even though they will miss their old treehouse, they were excited to build a new one. And they even learned what it meant to look at the bright side of things.

Endless Possibilities

Zoe, Jack, and Tom were three friends from three different families. Zoe was a fairy, Jack was an elf, and Tom was a dwarf. Tiny as these creatures were, they had big dreams. They were very clever, they loved to learn, and they never let others bring them down. One day, while hanging out, Jack asked his two friends what they wanted to be when they grew up.

Zoe said, "When I grow up, I want to be an explorer. I will lead a team of fairies to explore all over the world to find other fairy villages. Of course, I would have to work really hard and learn how to read maps so that I won't get lost. Then I will write a book about my travels so that young creatures can discover what is out there."

"That's an amazing dream, Zoe," Jack said. "How about you, Tom?"

Tom stood up proudly and said, "When I grow up, I want to be just like my dad. He is one of the best treasure hunters in our village and every night, he tells me stories about his adventures. My Dad and his team are responsible for keeping our village rich and bountiful. When I grow up, I will work with him. Then when he is too old to work, I will take his place as the leader of the treasure hunting team."

"That's so cool, Tom," Zoe said with admiration. "I know that you will be an amazing treasure hunter. You're so good at finding lost things!" This made Tom's smile grow bigger. Then he asked, "Now that you know our dreams, what do you want to be when you grow up, Jack?"

Zoe and Tom knew their elf friend very well. He was smart, kind, and helpful. With these traits, they knew that Jack could be a great leader of the elves. To their surprise, he said, "When I grow up, I want to become a teacher at our school?"

"Really?" Zoe asked. "We thought you would like to be something great like the leader of the elves."

"She's right," Tom agreed, "you're very smart and talented. You're a born leader too."

Jack smiled at his friends and said, "That's very kind of you. But being a teacher is a great dream too. As time goes by, I notice that young creatures are losing hope and ambition. When this happens, their futures won't be too bright. Look at you two. You both have amazing dreams because you grew up knowing that young creatures like us can be anything we want to be.

When I become a teacher, I will encourage my students to dream just like you. Then I will teach them how to work hard so that they can achieve those dreams."

"Wow," Zoe said, "you're right. That is a great dream, Jack. And it's true, even if we're still young, nothing should stop us from dreaming big. For us, the possibilities are endless!"

Conclusion: Storytelling Before Bedtime

With all of these stories to share, your child's bedtime routine will be richer and more relaxing. By sharing one story each night to your child, you will be sending them off to sleep and give them fantastic dreams to imagine. These stories come with valuable lessons but they do more than that. They will inspire your children to imagine, explore the world, and apply the things that they have learned during your bedtime storytelling adventures.

Even if you have already shared all of these stories with your child, you can keep going back to them. Ask your child which story they want to hear again or which character they want to hear a story about. This collection of stories went beyond the "common" mythical creatures as it introduced rarer creatures that you can describe to your children.

While reading, you may have noticed that your child asked you a lot of questions. You might have also noticed that many of the stories here have open endings. These stories give you a chance to ask your child what they think happened after. This is more than just a book of fairytales. It's a collection of stories that inspire learning, creativity, and the development of important values.

Leave the review

As an independent author with a small marketing budget, reviews are my livelihood on this platform. If you enjoyed this book, I'd really appreciate it if you left your honest feedback. You can do so by clicking the link below. I love hearing from my readers and I personally read every single review.

Printed in Great Britain
by Amazon